Nantala

A Jaydürian Adventure

Lilian Oake

This is a work of fiction. The characters, incidents and dialogues in this book are of the author's imagination and are not to be construed as real. Any resemblance to actual events or persons, living or dead, is completely coincidental.

No part of this book may be reproduced or transmitted in any form or by any means, electronic or mechanical, including photocopying, recording, or by any information storage and retrieval system, without permission in writing from the publisher.

Copyright 2017 by Lilian Oake - All Rights Reserved
Cover Art by Vlad Botos and Venkatesh Sekar.

Produced in U.S.A.

First Printing, 2017
Second Printing, 2018

ISBN-13: 978-1-7321265-0-3
ISBN-10: 173212650X

Dedication

To all my fellow artists, and those who have said
we won't get anywhere in life.
Neener, neener.
Neener.

Nahtaia
A Jaydürian Adventure

Lilian Oake

Table of Contents

Chapter 1	1
Chapter 2	13
Chapter 3	28
Chapter 4	39
Chapter 5	54
Chapter 6	68
Chapter 7	81
Chapter 8	93
Chapter 9	110
Chapter 10	120
Chapter 11	131
Chapter 12	143
Chapter 13	153
Chapter 14	160
Chapter 15	167
Chapter 16	178
Chapter 17	189
Chapter 18	197
Chapter 19	206
Chapter 20	218
Chapter 21	227
Chapter 22	238

x

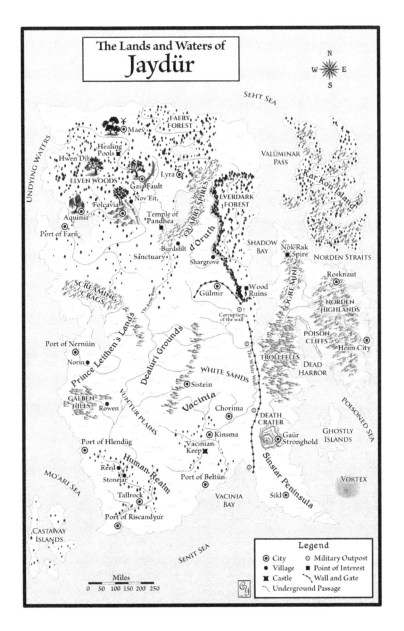

Chapter 1

The pine chair Nahtaia slouched on needed a good sanding. She would definitely have to replace her stockings after an hour of sitting on it. *I'm in trouble now*, she thought to herself, eyeing the larger chair on the other side of the desk—the desk belonging to Moriel, the Faery Forest's Minister of Fae Assignment.

It was the second time in four days that Nahtaia had been called for a meeting with Moriel. Last time, it was a scuffle with a local squirrel earning her the seat before the rather intimidating minister. She was not looking forward to his scolding gaze as she had already lost too much sleep to nervousness the memory of it caused."

The door creaked open behind her and Moriel entered. With a lump in her throat, Nahtaia watched as he made his way to the seat, his long white hair cascading down his back, smooth as silk. After taking his seat, he folded his hands, interlocking his slender, lengthy fingers and raised ivory eyes to hers.

The heart palpitations began. Those empty white eyes could bring anxiety up from the bravest of hearts. That's why they sent the bad little fae to him—because he could guilt trip a person just by making eye contact. It was his gift.

"Nahtaia," he began in a strong voice of composure. "Must I remind you at every meeting to bring your manners?"

Her brows raised with dumb curiosity.

"Ahem," he cleared his throat and sat up straight.

"Oh," she squeaked, straightening her back and pulling her feet together. "Sorry."

An exhausted sigh came from his pale lips. "Nahtaia, I called you here for a reason. It seems we're running out of—"

"It wasn't my fault!" Nahtaia blurted in defiance before he could go on. The all-knowing abysmal eyes of the minister were just too much. "That half-witted bull stepped into my ring!" she continued. "He ruined the perfect composition! I put so much hard work and focus into growing those mushrooms and he comes prancing about like a dunce!"

Moriel's jaw slowly dropped and his eyes widened. Nahtaia thought she even saw one of his eyelids twitch.

"You charmed a minotaur?" he croaked, nearly choking on the words.

Nahtaia paused and narrowed her eyes. "What exactly am I here for?" she asked, biting her nail.

Moriel dropped his face into his palms with a moan. "Oh, by the Highest. I was worried about the dog you turned into a pig, but *this*?"

Nahtaia's eyes brightened and she furrowed her brows. "Hey, that wretched animal nipped my wings! I had every right—"

"You shouldn't be in human territory in the first place! Just because you *can* use magic of such sorts does not give you the right to! Nahtaia, you..." Moriel stopped short. After taking in a deep breath of resignation, he continued. "Nahtaia, these meetings have become a habit I do not care to entertain. Your assignment was to keep watch over the forest's edge, not to go meandering into the neighboring farms. You know how much the humans detest faeries."

Nahtaia's wings flinched. That was not altogether true but she couldn't very well tell the minister that. He'd stare the truth out of her in a matter of seconds, and everyone knew what happened to faeries who wandered too far into human territory. Banishment.

Goosebumps rose all over her body at the thought of being denied any contact with Lyra. But even worse than that was the risk of losing her wings. Banishment wasn't simply cutting off a faery from her people; it was cutting off a faery from everything she was. No more magic. No more flight. Banishment was indeed harsh, but believed to be necessary when dealing with threats to the species. And approaching humans was practically inviting a threat. After all, history proved that humans caused the vast majority of faery deaths and homelessness.

"Nahtaia," Moriel snapped, drawing her out of her hollow gaze. "Are you listening to me? We have a final assignment for you, and if you fail or cause trouble of any sort, you will be punished most severely."

The seriousness in his eyes was also in his tone. Nahtaia swallowed hard. "What is the assignment?" she finally asked, tucking a long lock of blue hair behind her pointed silvery ear.

With that, Minister Moriel's lips curved into a contented smile and Nahtaia could feel the tension in the room lighten. "Something not even you can ruin, Nahtaia. Pine collecting."

There was only one reason he would suggest such a thing, and it boiled Nahtaia's blood to the surface. Her moon-pale face turned every shade of rose, from pink to blood-red. She jumped to her feet and clenched her fists, knowing in the back of her mind how ridiculous Moriel thought her reaction.

"Oren put you up to this, didn't he?" she accused, irritated by the very thought of the man with whom she'd knocked heads since childhood.

Moriel eyed the girl attentively. "With so much emotion coming from you, some would think you like the man," he said.

Nahtaia gasped in disgust, her hands curling into even tighter fists at her sides. "Blasphemy! He is an immature, selfish, poor excuse for a pine faery! I'd take up the company of a toothless goblin before liking him!"

"Oh, stop it, you're flattering me," another familiar voice spoke from behind.

Nahtaia turned. She hadn't heard the door or footsteps, but there was Oren with green goatee and snooty demeanor sitting in a chair behind her. His sleek, dark-green-tinted hair was pulled up into a ponytail, the bottom of which brushed against the rim of his brown tunic pants. A bow and quiver of arrows was slung over his bare back—obviously unused for quite some time as the arrows were neatly organized into a tidy bunch.

The moment her eyes set on him, her nostrils flared in fury.

"What's he doing here?" Nahtaia asked Moriel, though her spiteful glare remained on Oren.

Most girls were quite taken with Oren. He was not lacking in good looks, but his horrid personality and spoiled behavior greatly ruined that aspect. The chiseled lines and sharp angles of his face were often snuffed from thought when he opened his mouth.

"I'm here to take you to work, *Bluebird*," he said with a coy grin. "Funny how the world turns. I kept you out of trouble as a child, and here we find ourselves again."

Heat spread through her body as Oren spoke. Her bones showed through the knuckles of her fists, which she found difficult not to fling into his little olive nose.

"I refuse to do anything with this man," Nahtaia declared, turning back to Moriel. "This is absurd! You know very well, Minister Moriel, that nothing will get done if *he*," she jabbed a tiny finger at Oren, "and I are within sight of each other. I will not, nor will I ever, accept any assignment when—"

"If you're done with your tirade, Miss Nahtaia," Moriel cut in as he rubbed the inner corners of his eyes, "I have much work of my own to attend to. This is your assignment. You are to take direct orders from Oren Spindle from this moment on. Thank you. You know where to find the door."

He rose from his seat, took up some books and papers, then gracefully headed for the exit before he stopped and turned. "Oh, and don't think I've forgotten about the minotaur." With a deep sigh and shake of his head, he turned and disappeared through the door.

"Minotaur?" Oren snickered. "By the Highest, what have you done this time?"

Nahtaia stood, her eyes searching the wooden floor as if in it were hidden all the answers—and weapons—she desperately needed in this moment.

"Shut up," she snipped in reply.

Why was Oren *always* there? Since childhood, she couldn't seem to escape him. But at least he was never given any level of authority over her…until now. Now she was to take direct orders from him? Impossible. Inconceivable.

"Well, Bluebird, let's go," Oren continued, speaking closely into Nahtaia's ear. If she didn't know him so well, she would have recoiled at his closeness. But it was nothing new. When they weren't throwing punches or pinning one another down in a show of strength, their time was often spent just trying to make each other uncomfortable. And yet his voice sent a jolt of ice down her spine this time.

Nahtaia said nothing in return.

"All right, then. Take your time," he went on, taking a step back. "Honestly, Bluebird, this may not be so bad. We may actually have some—"

Without looking up, Nahtaia pushed past him with a puff. "I need some air."

"Fun," he finished.

Winter in Lyra, the largest city in the Faery Forest, was coming to an end. A slight chill still hung in the air, but with the thickening canopy, it was clear that spring was on its way. A myriad of flower buds sprang up through the thinning sheet of slick snow. Animals came out from hibernation with little cubs, kits, and chicks. It was time for the pine faeries to begin their work in the forest, collecting pine needles and cones to clear the ground for a new beginning.

Amid the fae, confidence rose within the citizens of Lyra with the unlikeliness of being seen by any passing travelers.

Nahtaia flew lower than most faeries—under the canopy instead of through it. That was another issue that often brought on scornful looks from her peers and unwanted attention from the ministers, but Nahtaia couldn't help it. There was a sense of freedom beneath the canopy that most of the fae were afraid to discover. Without the cover of leaves and branches, a faery was much easier to spot.

That sense of freedom, however, came to a sudden halt with the sound of Oren's voice.

"Nahtaia!" he called.

She clenched her teeth and narrowed her eyes, pushing herself to fly faster. But the moment Nahtaia's lips pulled up in a pleased smirk, thinking she got the better of him, Oren's fingers wrapped around her ankle and jerked her back. She turned and attempted to jerk her foot from his hold. But being an archer, his grip was strong.

"Thought you were too fast for me?" He chuckled.

"I *am* too fast for you," Nahtaia replied with a kick. He let go for an instant before snatching her wrist to pull her down to his eye level.

"Remember what Moriel told you," Oren said. Shadows reflected off his dark-green eyes, blackening them. "You take direct orders from me." He paused, moving an inch closer, spreading his grin to the point that dimples emerged. "I guess I can call you mine now."

Nahtaia's face burned, and her belly turned. Without any thought, and for maybe the hundredth time since they'd known each other, Oren's face became well acquainted with her fist.

"Don't you ever say that to me again, you putrid clump of dung mold!"

With Oren temporarily blinded, Nahtaia took off for the edge of the forest. She wore a proud smirk on her face, though in the back of her mind, she knew she would be punished for what she did. They weren't kids any longer.

"He deserved it," Nahtaia told herself, rubbing her sore knuckles. "No one talks to me like that."

When she reached the edge of the woods, Nahtaia slowed down and stopped in a large shrub. With her eyes on a human farm in the distance, she took a seat on a branch and let out a weary sigh as fear of the ministers set in.

What have you done? she thought to herself, leaning her head on a branch. Her knuckles started to pulse in pain.

Nahtaia remained there for a few minutes, watching horses and dogs wander the edge of the field that separated the human village from the faery forest. The shrub she sat in was where she always went to think. It was quiet, and no other faery dared go so far from home. Humans were dangerous, after all.

Nahtaia wondered what made her so much braver than the other faeries. "It's not bravery," she whispered the words other faeries had said to her, "it's called stupidity." Her heart fluttered with nervousness.

"So this is where you ran off to," Oren said, nearly startling Nahtaia off the branch.

She looked up at him with narrowed, angry eyes. With his hands braced against an upper twig, he stood with one leg casually crossed over the other. The left side of his face was swollen and red with a small patch of purple in the middle of the cheekbone. He dropped down to sit beside her.

"You didn't report me," she said.

"If I did, they'd lock you up," he replied with a grin. "Then I wouldn't be able to spend any time with you."

Nahtaia wrinkled her nose and forehead in disgust. "You don't get it, do you?" she said.

"What, that you despise me?" he replied, brows raised. "Oh no, I get it. But that only makes me like you more."

"Oh, stop it. No you don't."

Oren laughed. "I don't understand why you always think I'm lying."

"Because that's what you do," Nahtaia replied. "You lie and you flirt and you put on this show for attention."

Oren crossed an arm over his chest and lifted his other hand to his chin. He traced his jaw with the back of his fingers, as he often did when he was considering his next words.

"There's one way for you to know how I feel," he said, his voice suddenly quieter. "You can let me kiss you."

"Oh, please," Nahtaia said with a guffaw. "Go find a chipmunk and—"

Before she could finish her thought, the squeaking of a human cart was heard nearing. Nahtaia and Oren dashed to the back of the shrub and hid behind a denser bunch of leaves.

"Let's go," he whispered, taking her hand.

She jerked away and fixed her attention on the cart in wonder. An older man drove the contraption while two smaller humans sat in the back—a girl and a younger boy.

"Nahtaia, I know that look in your eyes. We have to go," Oren pressed. "We're already too far from Lyra's border. We'll have no help if you do something stupid."

"If you're so frightened, then go away," she hissed, glancing between him and the humans.

Oren pressed his lips in a tight line. "Nahtaia, you have to stop. You're putting yourself and the city of Lyra in danger by being here."

Nahtaia's breath hitched in her throat, and she briefly clenched her hands as she threw a glance over her shoulder. "You're just mad because I won't follow your orders."

Something in his eyes changed and his expression turned from concerned to glowering. "You've changed, Nahtaia. Don't you ever stop to think about consequences to your actions?"

His words made her stomach turn sour and her cheeks burn. She let her hair fall in between them. "Being stuck with you is consequence enough."

Oren tensed and shook his head. "That's it. Nahtaia, if you don't come with me now, I will report you, not only for the blow to my face, but for the danger you've put all of Lyra in by leaving the border."

Nahtaia snapped her attention to him and hatefully stared him in the face. Who did he think he was to threaten her like that? She would prove to him that his words didn't scare her in the least; he held no power over her.

"Do what you will," she snipped and in the blink of an eye, darted into the field toward the cart with one glance over her shoulder.

Fear and surprise twisted his face as he watched her shrink away from the safety of the forest and into the perilous human world.

Chapter 2

Clearly, Nahtaia was not thinking straight when she left Oren in the shrub. The moment she reached the wooden cart, the harsh voice of sense screamed a warning at her, but it was too late. The cart steadily bumped and thumped on the damp earth beneath it. Nahtaia fluttered underneath it, the only place no one would take notice of her glow.

Stupid, stupid girl, she said to herself, flying to the side of the wheeled contraption. A few rotted holes in the wood served as a solid grip. The instant she grabbed hold and stopped fluttering her wings, the glow diminished. *I'm sure to be banished now. If Moriel finds out about this, I'm as good as dead.*

Nahtaia's ears perked up at the sound of a human's laughter, and curiosity tugged once more at her little heart. With a quick lick of her lips, she pulled herself up just enough to see over the side of the cart. It was the girl. She held a small leather ball in her hand, but her attention was on a little boy beside her. She found it strangely entertaining every time he would puff up his cheeks or cross his eyes in an odd, ugly fashion.

"Humans," Nahtaia muttered, taking the opportunity to study them while she had the chance. With their rounded ears and asymmetrical faces, they just didn't seem to fit in the world. Even dragons and elves had some proportion. What strange beings.

Nahtaia let out a squeak of disapproval when the cart jolted to a stop. Her eyes quickly swept over the area, looking for a hiding place, anywhere the humans wouldn't see her. She spotted a small wooden stable that was only yards away. The human children were gathering their things to climb down—still giggling and chortling away—but the instant they both turned away, Nahtaia took her chance.

She pushed herself, flying as fast as her wings would take her, hoping her bluish glow wouldn't attract anyone's attention. The moment the three walls of the stable surrounded her, relief washed over her and she let out a pleased sigh.

"Bravo," she puffed with a grin.

Suddenly, something sounded from the outside and Nahtaia dropped to the floor with a gasp. The older man, the driver of the cart, was leading the horse in her direction, and she ran behind a bale of hay.

Fear crept over her at the thought of what the humans would do if they discovered her. She had to escape somehow and it had to happen right then. Nahtaia trembled in fear and squeezed her eyes tight in thought.

But another fear weighed heavily on her mind: if the ministers were to discover that a faery was seen in the town, they would know instantly that it was her. She was the only one mad enough to do such a thing. She had to be clever about her escape and do it well away from the eyes of the surrounding people.

I'll leave when they all go inside, she told herself.

"Grandfather," a feminine voice spoke, "can Willeim play in the hay?"

Nahtaia gasped in fear. She was behind the hay! Her mind spun with every possibility of escape—then it hit her. She could distort herself to look like a human.

I could fool them, she thought. *I could fool them into accepting me as one of their own!*

Without wasting another moment, she huddled on the floor and closed her eyes, calling the magic inside of her to distort her color and size to look as much like the girl from the cart as she could. Desperately hoping the magic worked right, she picked herself up and rose to her feet.

The man was looking at his horse with his back toward the hay bale Nahtaia hid behind, but the girl and little boy spotted her and shook in surprise.

"Hello," the girl said with bright, curious eyes.

The boy had a different reaction. His jaw dropped slightly and he slowly, yet deliberately, clung to his sister's arm. His eyes held more fear in them than surprise as he took a step back. Or were they suspicious?

The older human frowned and turned around. "Well, well," the old man said with a chuckle. "Where did you come from? Are you lost, little miss?"

Nahtaia's lips parted to speak, but it took a moment for her to make a sound. When she did reply, it wasn't without a horrid stutter.

"I-I-I'm sorry, s-sir," she said, swallowing hard. "Um, I, uh, w-was lost and cold and, um, it was warmer here."

In that moment, Nahtaia saw something she didn't expect. The old man's eyes crinkled with a kind smile. Wrinkles lined his face, and a faded reminder of the striking man he must have been when he was younger showed. His hair was short, white and disheveled, matching the strange tuft of hair that grew wildly from his chin. Nahtaia's fears slightly faded—a fact that surprised her.

His brow furrowed slightly and he pressed his lips in a tight line. "Are you from this village or traveling?" he asked, studying her tattered attire. Fear that she was inappropriately dressed as a human ebbed in and out of her mind. If the people had any suspicion, it would only be a matter of time before she was discovered.

"Traveling," Nahtaia replied.

The man thought for a moment before saying, "The town is an hour's walk back." He scratched his furry chin for a moment before letting out a deep breath. "Well, now that I've seen you, I can't let you leave dressed in such a way. You might attract negative attention." He turned to the girl. "Terralyn, fill up the basin and give her a change of clothes for her trip home."

Nahtaia looked down at her attire and frowned. She had on a brown shirt with loose stitches at the sleeves, pants that were much too large, and dirt caking her arms and face in patches. She remembered the image she had in her mind while distorting herself—tattered and poor, something to be pitied. The magic had worked well.

Terralyn nodded and stepped forward, smiling. "My name is Terralyn Mason, but you may call me Terry. All my friends do."

Nahtaia blinked in wonder. "Friends?"

"Yes," Terry smiled. "We can be friends. You're just about my age." She took Nahtaia's hand and led her toward the house. "Are you fifteen years old? Or maybe sixteen. What's your name, by the way?"

Nahtaia was in shock. The last thing she expected was to gain a human friend. Humans and faeries never got along. There was always a hatred between the species as humans continued to catch faeries for potions and things of that sort. Nahtaia couldn't deny that lingering sense of disgust for humans, but at the same time, she was fascinated by the creatures.

"Nahtaia," she replied, confused and wondering if it was wise for her to give Terry her real name.

"Nahtaia? That's pretty. I've never heard a name like that before."

The house was small and bright with the sunlight that shone through the windows. Chairs were spread strategically throughout the house so that one would always have somewhere to sit and rest. A delightful smell like Nahtaia had never experienced floated throughout the home, making her mouth water.

She had to get home as soon as possible. Not only was she in grave danger surrounded by humans, but she was hungry, too.

As Terry led her through the main hallway past other rooms, Nahtaia couldn't help but stare, wide-eyed, at every piece of decoration. It was nothing like a faery's home. There was no sign of nature, save for the wooden walls. A faery's home was full of flowers and petals and acorns and bark and anything one would find lying scattered throughout the woods.

The pair stopped before a door that Terry entered, then she turned with a frown.

"Willy," she sighed, "is there a problem?"

Nahtaia looked down at the little boy whom she didn't even realize was following them. There was something more than just his hair in his round blue eyes; there was an awareness of sorts, and it made Nahtaia edgy. His jaw hung slack, as it was the first time they saw each other in the stable, but he said nothing.

"Go tell Grandmama we have a guest and we'll be down shortly," she finished, then closed the door behind her. Looking up at Nahtaia, she giggled. "Don't worry about him," she said reassuringly. "He doesn't take kindly to strangers. In this case, though, I think he just finds you very pretty. I've never seen him ogle anyone like that before."

Nahtaia nodded, though a sense of foreboding tickled her senses. Trying to push the thoughts away, she stole a glance around the room. A large metal basin sat in the middle with towels. Odd wax blocks were stacked beside it, one atop another. A fair amount of light entered the room through the single window that faced the west.

"Here," Terry started, motioning to a chair in the corner of the room. "You sit while I fill the tub. It will take a few minutes."

Nahtaia took a seat and found herself wondering how she got herself mixed up in such an odd situation. There she was, in the middle of a human house, taking orders from a human! But caution was imperative and she wouldn't risk banishment for making contact with them. She had to be careful about her escape.

"You don't talk much, do you?" Terry said softly as she poured the last bucket of water into the basin. She had gone in and out of the home at least a dozen times, fetching water from someplace else.

Nahtaia blushed when Terry looked up at her.

"I just don't know what to say," she replied.

Terry nodded and smiled. "Don't you worry. My grandmother will have you well fed before you leave here, I can assure you, and maybe by then you'll be able to open up. We enjoy having guests, as scarcely as they come. Until you go, though, I really am glad to have another girl my age here for once. Living so far from the other villagers, it's hard to find anyone to talk to. How old did you say you were?"

"Sixteen winters," Nahtaia replied.

"Ah, as I thought." She motioned for Nahtaia to stand and helped peel off her clothes. "The water will only be warm for a little while, so we need to get started."

Nahtaia had never washed in such a way. She was used to springs and creeks and ponds—anywhere clean and hidden from human eyes. Nor was she used to having help, but Terry went on talking about friends from the town and just about anything else that came to mind while helping her scrub away the brown filth from her skin.

When they were finished, Nahtaia dressed in a blue peasant dress that fit her nearly perfectly. Her body type was much like Terry's: tall, slender, and lacking hips.

"Let us see what Grandmama has prepared for dinner," Terry said with a deep breath. "I'm famished."

Nahtaia followed Terry back down the hallway, then into a large main room, which Nahtaia learned was called a "kitchen." Faery homes didn't have kitchens.

"Grandmama!" Terry greeted a small robust, elderly woman with a hug.

"Hello, Terry," the woman replied with a warm smile.

Everyone is so nice, Nahtaia thought. She'd seen nice humans on her own secret expeditions but nothing like the people with her now.

"I want you to meet Nahtaia," Terry said, turning to face her. The woman smiled and surprised Nahtaia with a hug of her own.

"Hello, dear," she said. "My husband just finished telling me how he found you in the stable. I was just out there myself not moments before you arrived and I didn't see you. Poor thing. You should have said something."

Nahtaia didn't know how to reply. "I'm sorry," she managed in a small voice.

"That's okay, my dear. Come and have a seat. The potatoes are getting cold."

Nahtaia followed Terry to a large wooden table, wondering when an opportunity of escape would show itself. Within moments, the older man appeared from outside and after washing his hands, took a seat at the table. Little Willy followed close behind. The moment he spotted Nahtaia, his gaze was locked on hers and her stomach twisted uncomfortably.

The family was sharing events of the day between them when another human walked into the kitchen. Dropping a leather belt of tools beside the door, his eyes fleetingly met with everyone's before settling on hers.

"Hello," he said, nodding a greeting, his lips curved into a half-smile.

Nahtaia's cheeks warmed at his attention.

"Kale!" Grandmama greeted him as he washed his hands in a basin on a small corner table. "Welcome home. Come and eat. We have a guest."

"I see that," the boy named Kale replied. "I met Willy outside and he spoke of her. He insisted she is some sort of outlandish creature, but it seems he just lacks the sense to know natural beauty."

The warmth in her face turned to a radiating heat at the words spoken of her. Where she would normally be flattered, fear gripped her at the confirmation that Willeim was, after all, suspicious. But why? What could he see that the others could not?

The family laughed in unison, then Willeim jumped up from his seat with his brow deeply furrowed and his hands clenched into fists. "Don't you see it?" he asked. Nahtaia was surprised to hear him finally speak. That surprise quickly fragmented into horror when he pointed a finger at her and cried, "She's blue!"

All of the family turned at once to Nahtaia and frowned. She nearly sprouted her wings in that moment to flee.

"Willeim, stop this nonsense," Grandmama cut in. "Nahtaia is a guest in our home and will be treated as such."

Kale took the only empty seat beside Nahtaia and held out his hand.

"Hello again," he said. "It's a pleasure meeting you."

A knot the size of a finch blocked her throat as she took his hand in a shake. They could not see what Willeim saw. She wondered how that could be.

"Hello," she whispered. "Nahtaia. My name is Nahtaia."

The way he stared at her made her feel strange. There was something pleasant about him but at the same time, that sense of disgust for humans rose again at his touch. He wasn't unfortunate-looking. His brown hair was oddly shorter than she'd ever seen on a man, but his bright blue eyes were stunning in contrast with his sun-darkened complexion. It was just the fact that he was human that made her wish she could scrub her hands clean.

"Well," Grandfather cut in, "now that we're all acquainted, let us eat. I'm sure Nahtaia here is expected home soon."

Terry looked up at Nahtaia with a frown. "I wish you didn't have to go already," she said.

When Nahtaia turned her gaze to Terry, her eyes met once more with the wide, all-seeing eyes of Willeim and her skin prickled. *I wish I was gone now*, she thought before looking to Terry and replying, "I can always come back." The moment those words left her lips, she wanted to slap herself. Why she said it, she didn't know.

"Oh, please do!" Terry grinned.

"Where do you live?" Kale asked when he finished chewing a mouthful of food.

Nahtaia thought for a moment. "A few miles northwest," she replied. "Near the woods."

It wasn't a lie and yet, not the whole truth. How clever she felt.

With nods of their heads, everyone grew quiet as they finished up their meal. It was a strange meat that Nahtaia had never eaten before, but it was delicious.

When Terry and Grandmama rose and began clearing off the table and washing dishes, Kale turned back to Nahtaia.

"I've never seen you in these parts," he said, leaning his elbows on the table.

"I normally keep to my own territo—" she paused. "My own home. I like to be home."

Kale nodded and smiled. His expressions were increasingly kind and telling of the effort he put into absorbing her every word. Nahtaia couldn't help but notice everything about his face. Human men were so different from faery men. Their faces were round with dry, rough skin, whereas faery men had sharp, angular features and glowing, silky skin.

Nahtaia jumped when Grandfather's voice boomed as he spoke.

"Terry, Kale, will you show Nahtaia to the main road?" he asked. "Before it grows too late for her to safely travel."

Kale looked at Nahtaia with a smile and Terry took her hand, pulling her to her feet.

Fear and excitement rose within her at the thought of finally going home. Did the ministers even notice her absence?

"It was very nice having you, dear," Grandmama said, kissing her cheeks.

"Feel free to come by again," Grandfather added. "Terry lives a lonely life this far from the villages."

Nahtaia nodded and tried desperately to avoid Willy's gaze on her way out. After bidding their farewells, Nahtaia, Kale, and Terry made their way off into the distance.

Only moments passed when they reached a narrow dirt road that led off into the horizon. It was late afternoon and the air was cooler.

"Nahtaia," Terry began with a sigh, "please come back to visit soon. Even though you didn't say much, it was nice to have you here."

Nahtaia looked down at her dress and frowned. "Thank you, but what about the—"

"You can bring it back." Terry grinned in excitement. "A reason for you to return."

"I don't know when I can manage something like this again," Nahtaia admitted, exchanging glances between Terry and her brother. When Terry's eyes fell, she quickly added, "But I'll try. At least to return the clothes." After all, it would be the kind thing to do.

Nahtaia frowned at herself, wondering where the sudden desire to please this human girl arose from. To make things worse, a sense of gladness also appeared when Terry's face lit back up again.

"Well, I've only known you a short while," Kale started, "but I suppose we'll be better acquainted next time." Once again, he held out his hand and again, Nahtaia reluctantly took it.

Terry then took her up in a hug and they said their goodbyes. As Nahtaia started her way down the road, Terry and Kale returned to their home. The moment they were out of sight, Nahtaia shrank back into her natural size and form, dress and all, then flew back toward the woods. When she neared the edge of the forest, blood rushed from her face and turned cold as her eyes set on the line of faery sentries, armed and serious. Before them was Oren, armored with dark eyes and his arms crossed over his chest. She'd never seen him so legitimately angry.

Nahtaia stopped yards from them and Oren gradually closed the distance in between.

"Moon Faery Nahtaia," he said, his voice calm and composed, "Minister Moriel is waiting."

"I can't believe you told," Nahtaia huffed for the third time in the few moments they sat in Moriel's office.

"I told you I would," Oren replied from behind.

"You think I believed you?"

He let out a loud, long sigh and stood in front of her, leaning on the minister's desk. Nahtaia refused to look at him as she smoothed her hands over the wrinkling dress.

"It would be wise to start," he said. "Nahtaia, we're not kids anymore. Not everything is a joke."

Before he could go on, the door opened, revealing an angry Minister Moriel. One look at the dress Nahtaia wore, and his jaw clenched. There was a stiff, controlled air to his walk, as if using every bit of strength not to explode into a fit of rage.

He sat down and folded his hands as he always did, then raised empty eyes to Nahtaia.

Her anger at Oren's big mouth diminished her usual fear of the minister, and she didn't even return his gaze.

"I know," she started. "I'm in trouble. I failed the assignment and you've run out of options for me." Finally looking up, her eyes met with Oren's instead of Moriel's. "Thanks a lot," she muttered.

With that, Oren bristled and his eyes widened as he straightened his back. "What did you expect me to do?" he asked through clenched teeth, dropping his hands to his sides. "I didn't know if you were ever coming back!"

Nahtaia crossed her arms more tightly. "So what if I didn't? You and those sentries would come out looking for me?" She let out a skeptical huff. "Spare me."

"Don't give me that—"

"Run to the ministers when I do something a little out of line."

"A little?"

"Stop this bickering," Moriel cut in. "If it weren't for Oren, you'd be banished a hundred times over already. He is an honorable man—something every man in Lyra should strive to be."

Nahtaia rolled her eyes.

"Thanks to him," Moriel continued, "you still have your wings."

That got her attention, though not without great suspicion. "What do you mean?" she asked, her gaze drifting curiously to Oren. He was suddenly biting his bottom lip, forcing back a smile. "Oh, no." This was going to be bad. "Tell me."

"Oren now has a new assignment," Moriel said. With that wicked half-smile that was so well known throughout Lyra, Moriel bore his smug gaze into hers. "You."

Chapter 3

The silence in Minister Moriel's office was excruciating. Nahtaia tried to hold back her anger, she really did, but the desire to unleash her wrath on any breathing creature near her won the battle.

"Are you insane?" she shrieked. "This is madness! Did someone put a pinch too many poppies in your morning tea?"

Moriel threw an "I told you so" look at Oren, who grinned widely in return. Nahtaia didn't know what to do with herself, and her mouth opened and closed in silent protest.

"He offered himself for the job, and I thought it an appropriate punishment for you, considering your relationship. He knows you well. There is no getting out of this one." Moriel stood up from the desk and walked to a window looking out into Lyra's city streets below them. "He will shadow you. Everything you do, everywhere you go, he will be there to watch you. He is to report any nonsensical actions or abuse to me daily and the appropriate consequence will be received by you, willingly."

From her peripheral view, Nahtaia saw Oren step up beside her. Her heart thumped at his closeness.

Shadowing? If she had known that to be the consequence, she would never have gone to the humans. Nothing was worth this. But no, that was the situation and decisions had been settled. There was no chance of escape.

A silence fell over the room as Nahtaia took in the information. A cold, horrendous silence seeped through her flesh and crawled beneath her skin like a parasite. A future shackled to Oren? No. It couldn't be. She wouldn't have it.

In the blink of an eye, Nahtaia seized the dagger in Oren's boot and dropped to the floor on her knees in a dramatic show that brought out a surprised cry from the minister.

"Do it!" she cried from the floor, one hand clutching her chest while offering Moriel the dagger in her other hand. "Just do it! Take my wings, for any fate would be willingly accepted more than this!"

The men stared down at her with wide eyes, completely caught off guard by Nahtaia's reaction.

"Well, there goes what's left of my ego," Oren scoffed.

Nahtaia stayed on the floor, waiting for Moriel to do something—to say something—but he simply pressed his fingers to his temples.

"Nahtaia," he began, "this dramatic show is doing nothing but making me worry about your mental health. Now get up."

Nostrils flared and teeth clenched, she stood up. The dagger clattered to her feet and Oren knelt to pick it up.

"As exciting as all this really is," he began, tucking the dagger back into his boot, "I'd really like to get a feel for my new assignment."

The moment his hand found the small of her back to guide her out of the office, Nahtaia tensed.

"You will refrain from touching me with those mangy claws of yours unless you desire being a dung beetle for the rest of your life."

Oren curled his fingers back and gestured toward the door. "After you." Nahtaia spun on her heel, then fluttered out the door. Oren followed Nahtaia and turned to nod respectfully to Minister Moriel, who shook his head as the door closed.

The streets of Lyra were still alight with fae traveling to and fro. Faeries of every kind were about, but Nahtaia couldn't be bothered with conversation. She was angry and humiliated. Of all the punishments she'd ever received in her sixteen winters of life, being shadowed by Oren was by far the worst.

"Nahtaia," Oren's voice was heard, no more than a whisper beneath the objections and curses that screamed in her mind. "Nahtaia. Nah-ty," he began in an irritating, singsong voice. "I know you can hear me. You know, your silence only makes me enjoy this more. It brings a little more suspense to the situation. 'When will Nahtaia first speak?'" he said in a deep, exaggerated voice. "'What will be Nahtaia's first words?'"

He followed her through the city streets as he amused himself with one-way chatter. When they finally reached Nahtaia's home—a small wooden hollow embellished with stones and glass found in the surrounding woods—they stopped before the door. The fluttering sound from Oren's translucent wings stopped. Nahtaia stared at the door in thought. Was he to intrude upon her home as well? Would she be denied even the smallest bit of privacy?

"Nahtaia," Oren said. It was obvious by his voice that he was still grinning.

"I need a moment to myself," she replied, her face to the door. "Just a moment to think."

Oren sighed and reached his arm just above her shoulder, then pushed the door open. He leaned down into her ear and said, "Just a moment."

With a nod, Nahtaia stepped into her home. The moment the door clicked shut behind her, she licked her lips and smiled. Darting to a back window, she slowly and carefully opened it, turning to listen for any movement on the other side of the door. All was silent, so she climbed out of the window and closed it. With a sigh of victory, she smoothed out her hair, then turned to be on her way. She immediately bumped into Oren.

"I find it hard to believe that you actually thought that would work," he chuckled, putting an arm around her shoulders. "That was the worst attempt at escape I've ever seen."

Nahtaia growled in frustration and shoved him off.

"You frog-legged, bee-hinded, mangy mound of cow-cud!" she yelled in his face.

"You're really good at that," he noted.

"Of all the horrible things you've done to me, you could not have chosen anything worse!"

"Oh please, besides trying to help you get out of banishment, what have I done?" Oren scoffed.

Nahtaia laughed incredulously. A million situations easily leaped to mind. "What about the time you pulled me into the beehive down by Silver Lake?"

Oren furrowed his brow. "I fell back."

"You did not!"

"After you threw a leech at me!"

"Don't exaggerate, it was a worm."

Oren's eyes widened. "It was a leech! It took an hour for me to finally convince it to let go! I still have the scar," he said through clenched teeth, pointing to a fading white scar beside his left ribs.

Nahtaia bit her lip and narrowed her eyes. "That's not my fault."

Oren threw his arms up in disbelief. "You're unbelievable. You're *childish.*"

To Nahtaia's surprise, Oren's words stung. She turned away, stubbornly crossing her arms over her chest as she fluttered back through the window. It took a moment for Oren to recompose himself before he chuckled. Nahtaia frowned and shot him a curious gaze as he climbed in behind her.

"What is so funny?" she asked.

"You're good," he replied with a shake of his head. He started toward the door. "You're really good. You think you'll rid yourself of me if you drive me crazy enough. I'll be just outside, along with my sentries—all night—waiting for you to wake."

Nahtaia watched Oren as he left her home, then slammed the door in his face.

"Good night, Bluebird," he called from the other side.

Crickets chirped from below the canopy and a wind was blowing in from the east. Peaceful as it was, the night passed gruesomely slowly for Nahtaia. The fact that sentries guarded her home's exits did not make it any easier.

"This is absurd," she muttered. "Of all the stupidity."

Suddenly one of the men snored at such an impressive volume, the windows rattled, and they continued clattering with each breath. Nahtaia sat up in bed, startled, then made her way to a window. She slowly pulled back the curtain and peeked through the glass.

There he was. The pine faery Fromm's enormous figure, slumped on the ground. Nahtaia grinned. Darting to the door and looking through the smaller window beside it, she saw the other sentry was gone…but she could hear his footsteps around the farther end of her home.

Without so much as a second thought, she grabbed Terralyn's dress and was out of the house and flying below the canopy. She would return the dress as she said she would. Though she knew that she'd get in trouble again for running away, the thought of being far from Oren's men was enough to give her the boost she needed to risk it. Either way, what fate was worse than living with Oren a step behind?

It was early morning and the sun was still down. Most animals were yet in their dens, but for the owls. Nahtaia had already passed the safe barrier and would have to keep a keen eye out for them, lest she lose more than just her wings. Alas, her eyes were not so keen.

A screech echoed through the forest, not far from her. Nahtaia stopped mid-flight to extinguish her glow, dropping to a shrub on the ground.

"Someone will have heard that," she told herself.

She scanned the trees above for any sign of the owl when its resounding screech rang out once more, soon followed by the sound of feathered wings on air.

"Curse it!" she growled as she flew up from the shrub and into the thickest part of the canopy. With a quick glance behind, she spotted the owl's round yellow eyes focused intently on her. She pushed herself harder toward the largest tree she could find and spotted a hole just big enough for her to fit.

By the Highest, please be deeper than you look! she thought in a panic.

Her mind spun, making distortion too dangerous to risk. Without the right focus, anything could happen with magic.

Nahtaia squealed with alarm when the owl nipped at her feet. Her wings began to tire, but there was no choice but to push harder. The hole in the tree was so close, and when she finally reached it, relief overcame her, though not for long. The hole was not as big as she'd hoped, and though the owl couldn't fit through, its beak reached just an inch away from her.

The bird thrashed against the tree, and with her back against the wall, Nahtaia could do nothing more than kick at it in defense. The edges of the hole began to crack and crumble—it would only be a matter of time before the bird reached its meal.

"Go away, you feathered rat!" she cried, kicking its beak once more. "I refuse to die this way!"

The owl was having a difficult time flying and pecking at the same time, but it pounded its head into the hole until a large piece of bark fell, giving the bird enough room to pluck her out. Nahtaia screamed as it lunged toward her once more, but both faery and owl startled when a whistling sound cut through the air and a small arrow flew into the side of the bird's neck.

The owl pulled back, shaking its head vigorously in an attempt to pull free from the arrow. Another arrow stuck beside the first. Nahtaia watched in wonder and disgust as blood spurted from the wounds. In a matter of seconds, the owl was dead at the foot of the tree.

Nahtaia crawled to the edge of the hole and looked at the creature below, then noticed the glow of a faery from the corner of her eye. She looked up and groaned when realization hit her. Jumping from the hole, she sped toward the bird and landed on its carcass.

"Wake up! I've changed my mind!" she shouted, grabbing and shaking its feathered neck. "Stupid bird, eat me!"

Oren seized her arm and pulled her to her feet, though it was no easy task. Nahtaia fought against his hold, pulling, fluttering, and digging her nails into his arms.

He shouted in pain, then jerked her to a stop, face to face. "For the love of all that's pure in this world, calm down!"

"Let me go!" she ordered, more quietly but with just as much resistance.

"Forget it," he replied. "We need to talk."

"No."

Nahtaia hovered and pressed her feet against his chest, pushing with all of her strength until he lost his grip on her arm. The instant she was free, she made her way to the edge of the woods with Oren close behind.

The edge of the forest came into view as well as the sun-kissed horizon. It was a breath of fresh air from the dark, bird-filled forest.

"Don't do it," Oren called, his face suddenly not so smug. "Nahtaia, please!"

But Nahtaia continued until she reached a field near Terralyn's home. She refused to let Oren feel any kind of control over her. He would not have the satisfaction. She would bear any other consequence besides him.

When she touched the edge of the field, Oren sped up and caught her by the wrist, twirling her to face him.

"What do you think you're doing?" he cried. "Don't you realize this is what got you into this mess in the first place?"

"*You* got me into this mess," she countered, her lips trembling. She didn't know why she was having this reaction or why the entire ordeal had her blood pumping more than she had ever known. "And I will not stand for it."

Oren scoffed. "You're the one who won't just follow directions."

She tried to pull away, snarling through clenched teeth, "I will respect those who deserve it, not any self-righteous fool who thinks himself higher than he is."

Instead of letting go, he seized her other wrist and jerked her forward until she stood so close, his breath warmed her face.

"You flatter me," he replied.

"Goodbye, Oren."

A line creased in his brow as she grew and grew. He lost his grip on her wrist and his eyes widened as she distorted into a human likeness.

"Nahtaia!" he cried. "Nahtaia, don't do this! You're being foolish! The ministers will have you killed if you bring any more trouble to Lyra! I demand you to return to your normal size!"

As her size grew, she felt her frustration with Oren shrink. Her lips pulled up as he hovered at eye level, again spitting out his demands.

"Oh, Oren. 'I demand this. I demand that,'" she mocked. "You are such a sore." She swatted him away and started toward the human home.

"Nahtaia!" he called. "The ministers will have you killed!"

She turned with a half-smile and put her finger to her lips. "Not if you don't tell."

Chapter 4

Oren darted around her face in all directions and Nahtaia swatted at him as if he were a pesky fly. When her patience ran thin, she turned to give him one more warning, but he'd suddenly disappeared. Nahtaia let out a contented sigh and turned, then gasped when she saw Kale on the road ahead of her.

"Hello," he said with a smile as he made his way to her. He hitched his belt of tools onto his shoulder and rubbed his hand on his pants before tipping his floppy gray hat to her.

"Hello," Nahtaia replied. "I'm sorry to intrude, but I was just returning your sister's dress."

"It's no intrusion," he said. "I have to admit, I didn't expect to see you again so soon, but it's a pleasant surprise. Especially so early."

Nahtaia blushed at his comment and nervously tucked a strand of her faux-brown hair behind her ear.

"I'm sorry, did I offend you?"

Nahtaia was surprised at his genuine kindness. It made it difficult for her to dislike him for being human as she had the previous day.

"Not at all," she replied. "I just never really know what to say to people."

"Yes, I am still a stranger, aren't I?" He chuckled, then glanced fleetingly at his home. "My sister is yet sleeping. This is normally the morning she has extra time to rest, so it will be a few more hours."

Nahtaia eyed his tool belt and apparel in wonder. She'd never seen tools like his, forged and shaped from metals. Faery tools were stone and wood; much less reliable, but they got the job done.

"I'm going to work for the day," he explained, noticing her interest. "I'm a stone carver. I'm currently working on a statue for one of the lords in the high country."

When he saw the confused expression on Nahtaia's face, he laughed and looked up the road. There was something in his eyes. A sense of nervousness, as if afraid to say what he intended to.

"W-would you like to see?" he asked, turning back to her. The corner of his lips twitched, making it obvious he was anxious about her response.

"To see your statue?" she asked.

He nodded. "If you're willing and have the time, that is. My workplace is not far."

He gestured up the road with one hand and offered her his elbow. She looked at it for a moment, then threw a quick glance behind, wondering if Oren was still watching her. With a lick of her lips, she accepted Kale's offer and joined him on his walk to work.

How odd it was being so close to him. There was still part of her mind reminding her that he was no more than a useless human, but she felt a sense of adventure spending time with him. Anyone who knew Nahtaia also knew that adventure was something she could not resist. *Or maybe*, she thought, *it is just stupidity*.

"Do you often wander by yourself?" Kale's voice broke through her thoughts as they made their way up the hill.

"Yes," she replied, glancing up at him, then back to the road. "I like to be alone."

"Why?"

"Um," she paused. "People aren't the nicest to me. I would rather spend time alone than suffer ridicule for being who I am."

Kale looked down at her in wonder. "Well, tell me, Nahtaia. Who are you?"

Her gaze fell to the side, away from his attentive eyes. "I'm just not like most girls."

Kale, seemingly aware of her discomfort with his question, quickly tried to change the subject. "Do you have family nearby?"

Nahtaia thought on that for a moment. Her parents disappeared when she was young; they were among the many fae who were caught by a traveling witch seeking out faery wings for her potions. They were gone and she had no siblings. But as she grew, she came to think of her community as a sort of family, even if they didn't get along most of the time.

"Yes," she finally replied. "They live on the other side of the woods."

"Ah," he said.

Nahtaia looked up at him from the corner of her eye. Kale was nearly a foot taller than she was, and he had a kind face; that much she did not deny. He and his siblings looked very much alike, and she could imagine little Willy growing to look even more like him.

"You're a lot like Terry," he added. "I think you two will get along very well. She also has trouble with her peers. They don't like her because she is smarter than them. What do they claim against you?"

Nahtaia couldn't help but laugh at her own answer, and that brought a handsome smile to Kale's face. A handsome human? Who'd have thought it?

"What?" he asked.

"They say I'm too wild," she confessed with a smirk. "And too adventurous."

Kale's eyes widened. "I find that hard to believe. You've hardly spoken a word in the short time I've known you. Whatever I *have* heard has not been easy to worm out of you, either."

She couldn't help but giggle at the thought. It was true. She hadn't said much until then, while back at home, they claimed no one could make her stop talking. It was the fear of being discovered, she told herself. She was not afraid of humans as a species but of humans as enemies of Lyra. Though full of boring, judgmental, and irksome faeries, it was still her home.

The pair reached the top of the hill that overlooked a small marketplace. Tents sheltering wares and clothing from the weather spotted the area for half a mile. Red and blue flags blew in the air high above, and store signs squeaked with every slight breeze. Trees were sparse—likely chopped down for the purpose of building the market—and the sun peeked over the horizon, splaying rays of light up into the clouds.

Kale led Nahtaia to a large building made of red brick. He took a key from his pocket and unlocked the door, motioning for her to enter. "A merchant from one of the bigger towns nearby owns this place and allows me to use it, as long as I pay him a portion of my profit with every project."

"That's kind of him," Nahtaia replied as she stepped inside.

The building was empty, but for scattered tools and bales of hay lining the walls. There were small windows cut high up through the brick and one large one that let in most of the light. Beside that window stood a nearly finished statue of a nobleman.

Nahtaia went to get a closer look and found herself rather impressed. Every tiny detail in the man's stance and clothing was carved. His face was as smooth as the inside of a cut granite stone and with such chiseled features, it looked more like a real person than a lifeless statue. The eyes and facial features were perfectly carved down to the pronounced hook nose. Even the hair was delicately carved into curls.

"What do you think?" Kale asked, stepping up beside her. "And be honest."

"It's beautiful!" Nahtaia replied in shock. "I've never seen anything like it. This used to be a stone?"

Kale nodded. "A huge hunk of rock. The hardest part was moving it here and getting it inside."

"How long did it take you?" she asked, walking around the statue to take in every detail.

Kale furrowed his brow in thought for a moment. "It's been nearly a month now."

Nahtaia gasped. "Only a month?"

She looked up to find Kale staring at her with a strange softness in his eyes. In her own self-consciousness, she took a bit of hair that fell over her shoulder and nervously fiddled with it.

"Um," Kale cleared his throat and looked back to the statue. "Yes, a month. I'm not as fast as the best stone carvers but certainly quicker than others."

"To do this," Nahtaia gestured to the stone man, "in a month is quite a feat, in my opinion."

"In that case, I'll accept it as a compliment."

Nahtaia smiled and looked on in wonder as Kale gave her an in-depth explanation and even a demonstration of his work. When he noticed how curious and interested she really was, he showed her the tools and told her stories, some scarier than others, of accidents and wounds he'd received over time. Talk of his work eventually sparked talk of life in the human city not four miles from his home, called Corlan. He spoke of his family and his parents, who had died years before from a sickness that plagued the town. He was thirteen years old when it happened and went with Terralyn and Willeim to live with their grandparents.

Hours had passed and early morning eventually faded into the shadows of early evening. The pair only noticed when the sun fell below the windows, casting dark shadows on the walls and statue.

"Where did the day go?" Kale laughed, throwing a hand to his head. "Incredible. And all this time I've just blabbered on and on."

"You didn't blabber," Nahtaia smiled. "I enjoyed this day more than I expected. I mean, normally I don't loiter around people longer than an hour because I'm easily bored, but today I was really, genuinely—" she paused, catching herself turning back into the talkative faery everyone knew. She didn't want Kale to see that part of her. Most people didn't like it and who knew what truths she'd accidentally reveal if she didn't pay proper attention. "Genuinely interested," she shyly finished, dropping her gaze to the stone floor.

"I'm glad," Kale said with a smile.

An awkward silence rose between them for a moment.

"I think it's time—" Nahtaia started to say. At the same time, Kale said, "Would you—"

"Oh," he blushed, looking up through his long lashes. "You first."

"No, you started," she laughed.

"Oh, well, would you like to join me and my family for dinner? I've kept you here all day and it would only be proper for me to make sure you're fed before the day's end."

Nahtaia's smile faltered slightly at the thought of being in the same room with Willy and all those humans again.

"Oh, I don't know," she started. "If you could just give the dress…"

"My grandparents would love to have you," he cut in. "And of course, you know Terry will be elated. Even Willy. He seems to have some sort interest in you. A crush of sorts," he laughed. "Please?"

The eagerness in his eyes was so obvious, and Nahtaia wondered if he realized it. She wasn't sure how good of an idea it was to see Willy again, but at the same time, she did still have to return Terry's dress. Maybe she did the magic wrong before. Maybe Willy wouldn't notice anything different this time. It took her a moment and another pressing plea from Kale before she finally accepted the offer and joined him on the walk home.

The sun was still above the winter-capped mountain peaks and trees. The air was chilly, which was expected since it was still early on in the year. Nahtaia gladly took the elbow Kale offered and clung to it a bit tighter than she would have if the weather was more agreeable. Which was odd, considering the fae did not feel hot or cold. The magic working for the guise was potent indeed. Kale did not seem to mind.

"I'd offer you my coat if I'd remembered to bring it," he laughed.

"It's all right," she replied as her eyes wandered into the line of trees at the edge of the forest. Was Oren still there? Would he be in the company of sentries when she returned?

When they reached the house, Kale opened the door for her, then followed her inside.

"Why, hello," Grandmama clapped happily from beside a pot in the fireplace. She quickly shuffled her way around the table and warmly hugged Nahtaia.

"Hello," Nahtaia replied. She was surprised to find that she was actually pleased to see the home and even Grandmama.

"Terry!" she called. "See who's come to visit!"

In less than a moment, Terralyn entered the kitchen and gasped in surprise when she saw Nahtaia.

"Hello!" she said, taking her up into her own hug. "Oh, I was afraid you wouldn't be coming back at all!"

"What's all the ruckus?" Grandfather asked from outside just before he entered the home. "Oh, welcome back. Nahtaia, is it?"

"Yes," she nodded. "I've come to return Terry's dress."

"And she's come with Kale, from the looks of it," Grandmama added. "Or did you just meet outside? I doubt it, since I first spied her walking to our house early this morn."

Nahtaia blushed and Kale scratched his head as he tried to think of an explanation. Grandmama's side of the story was enough for the rest of the family to come to their own conclusions.

"I suspect you're hungry," Grandmama changed the subject, motioning for everyone to take their seats at the table. Kale took the same seat he had the night before, beside Nahtaia.

"So this whole day has been spent with Kale?" Terry sighed, slightly annoyed. "Really, you couldn't say hello?"

"I'm sorry," Nahtaia said. "I didn't realize how the time was passing." She really did feel bad for not spending time with the girl. She enjoyed her company immensely the day before, when she thought of it.

"Well, I claim the rest of the evening with you—until you have to leave, that is," Terry smiled. "Are we in agreement?"

Nahtaia nodded and looked sidelong at Kale. "We are."

"Where is that little troublemaker of a boy?" Grandfather puffed. "When you don't need him, he's tripping you and causing all the chaos in the world, but when it's time for him to come home, he's nowhere to be found. Willeim!"

Nahtaia shook in surprise at Grandfather's call. Terry and Kale noticed and stifled their laughter, as they were used to the boom in their grandfather's voice.

Running footsteps came from outside and Willy threw the door open. "I'm here!" he said, winded, then froze when he set eyes on Nahtaia. "U-um," he stuttered. "I-I need to wash up." Before anyone managed to say a word to him, he disappeared into the washroom.

So much for not getting noticed, Nahtaia thought. She couldn't understand why he could see what others could not.

"He's taken quite a liking to you," Terry whispered over the table.

"It's just a little crush," Grandmama chuckled. "It's harmless."

Nahtaia eyed the hall where Willy ran. *Right*, she thought. *Just a crush.*

When Willy walked back into the room and took his seat, he was quite the unhappy little boy with eyes narrowed and accusing. Nahtaia didn't like it. Who was he to judge her? He didn't know her.

Dinner was, once again, delicious and completely new to Nahtaia, though hard to enjoy with the prying eyes of the wicked little boy. He *was* wicked. He had to be. She'd decided by the second forkful of food, when she realized he was still staring at her like a bug to be squashed. How dare he? But to her relief, when everyone was finished, Terry was quick to snatch her away. Nahtaia looked back to Kale, who seemed as if he would say something, but then waved disappointedly as she was dragged away by his sister to the bedroom.

When Terry closed the door behind them, she motioned for Nahtaia to sit. "You don't know how pleased I am to have you here again," she began. "If only for a short time."

Nahtaia didn't know how to reply.

"Tell me, how did you and Kale spend the day?"

"He showed me his work," Nahtaia said.

"And?"

"And we talked." She nervously fiddled with her hair again.

Terry frowned. "That's it? He didn't take you into town?"

"Is his work not in town?"

Terry laughed and shook her head. "He's on the outskirts of the marketplace. Hardly town. You mean to tell me the entire day was spent at his workshop?"

Nahtaia nodded. "Is that wrong?"

"Just deathly boring."

"I found it rather interesting."

She wasn't lying. Faeries didn't have stone statues; there was no reason for them, so the concept was new to her. Of course, anything new was interesting.

Another hour fluttered by in quiet conversation about their day and Nahtaia noticed herself opening up a lot more to Terry. With Terry's subtle encouragement, Nahtaia shared her own ideas on friends and boys, though, of course, she left out anything faery-related.

"Do you have your eyes on any men?" Terry leaned in and whispered with an excited grin.

Nahtaia frowned. "Not really."

That answer disappointed Terry as she wrinkled her brow with pursed lips. "No one?" she pressed. "No men in your life showing interest or who've gained your interest?"

Nahtaia thought for a moment. A rising anger came with the thought of Oren and all the times he'd ruined any interesting conversation she'd had with a man, but she decided not to make him a topic of conversation.

Terry looked at Nahtaia and smiled, then dropped her eyes to the floor. "What about my brother?" she said, fumbling with the corner of her dress.

Blood and heat rose to Nahtaia's face. "W-what?" she asked, swallowing hard.

Terry laughed and shook her head. "I'm sorry. You don't have to answer that. I know, it's too soon."

Nahtaia's mind raced. Was that really the idea everyone got about her and Kale? She'd hardly known them! Not to mention the fact that they were humans. Sure, she found Kale kind and sweet and more sufferable than anyone else, but she recognized where the issue would lie if they were to get *too* close.

Terry turned the conversation to more comfortable subjects from then on. When the sun was nearly gone and the time had come to leave, Nahtaia confidently called Terry her friend. There was no one in Lyra quite like her, and she realized that she'd take up conversation with her sooner than any faery she knew.

"Promise me you'll come again," Terry whispered in Nahtaia's ear as she hugged her goodbye, just outside the front door. "Promise me."

"I promise," Nahtaia replied.

"Nahtaia." Kale nervously smiled as he stepped forward, scratching his head. "I enjoyed your company today."

"And I enjoyed yours," she replied.

Another awkward moment passed before he held out his hand. Nahtaia took it, uncertain as to what he meant to do with it, then blushed as he kissed her fingers.

The family behind him exchanged smiles, and Grandmama motioned for Terry to get back inside the house. Kale's face turned scarlet as the door closed behind him.

"Uh," he began again. He seemed oddly nervous. "There is something I'd like to ask you before you go."

Nahtaia raised her eyebrows in curiosity, waiting for him to continue.

He cleared his throat. "I'd very much like to see you again."

"I'd love to come again," she replied excitedly. "I've never seen anything like your statue. It's incredible."

A grin spanning ear to ear spread on Kale's face and his words came more confidently. "What is the likelihood of you coming back tomorrow?"

Nahtaia thought for a moment. There was no way to know what awaited her back home. She was really in for trouble this time. Her heart anxiously skipped a beat, and she quickly pushed aside the thoughts of what would happen if she simply didn't return to face the ministers.

"I'm not sure," she replied. "I can try but I don't know the likelihood."

"As long as you try."

The pair said their final goodbyes and Nahtaia turned toward the edge of the forest.

"Are you sure you'll be all right?" Kale called, concern wrinkling his features.

"Yes," she called back. "I know my way. Thank you."

Kale waved once again and when she entered the forest, he went inside. Nahtaia stopped and took a deep breath.

"Here we go again," she whispered, then changed back into her faery self.

Chapter 5

When Nahtaia neared the forest's edge, she was surprised—and relieved—to find that Oren was nowhere in sight; no one was. She entered the forest slowly and attentively but there was no sign of life, so, with a pleased sigh, she swiftly made her way home.

The forest was quiet and darkening, bringing back unwanted memories of the owl attack earlier in the day.

Maybe I should travel as a human until I reach the safe-barrier, she thought. When she heard a loud rustling from within the canopy, she took a breath and changed, though she kept her wings to fly the rest of the way. The moment Lyra was within her sights, she shrank back and hurried to her home.

It wasn't dreadfully late, so many fae were still on the pathways of the tree city, but Nahtaia didn't have the time nor the patience for them. She wanted to sleep and go back to the humans. When once she loathed them and found them disgusting, she now found herself more fascinated than ever.

As she neared her home, she saw no glow in the area. That made Nahtaia wonder with a quiet whisper of suspicion.

Was Oren up to something? Did he really let her get away with the day?

The moment she reached her door, a smile flirted at the corner of her mouth. She entered her home, lit a candle, and turned to get ready for bed.

"Welcome home, Bluebird," Oren's voice spoke from the darkness.

Nahtaia shrieked with shock and jumped back, bumping into a table and knocking it over. The candle blew out and left her in darkness with her uninvited visitor. He was sitting on a chair in the far corner of the room, his eyes eerily brightened by the moon.

"By the Highest Power!" she squealed. "What is wrong with you? What are you doing in my house?" She leaned over and relit the candle while Oren jumped to his feet and shook his head. He did not look pleased. Nahtaia watched with caution as he slowly made his way to her.

"My patience is wearing thin, Nahtaia," he said with a scowl. His frustration was clear by the tightening of the muscles in his jaw.

"There were no sentries," she said, holding fast to her place. Did he think himself intimidating?

He dropped his gaze while a corner of his lips curved up into a forced half-smile. "I didn't turn you in," he said with an unexpected touch of shame to his tone.

Nahtaia furrowed her brow. "Really?" She paused. "That's oddly kind. Why not?"

He let out a disbelieving laugh and shrugged, unable to find his words. "I—"

There was a heaviness in the atmosphere. Nahtaia couldn't quite put her finger on what it was. She watched Oren as he smoothed the small tuft of hair on his chin with a sigh; she noticed that he wouldn't make eye contact.

"I'm going back tomorrow," she said, to her own surprise. Why she would openly admit such a thing, she did not know. "And you're not going to stop me."

His eyes finally snapped up to hers.

"Back?" he growled. "You mean, back to that boy?"

Nahtaia instantly bristled. A shadow of threat hung over Oren, and she felt the need to protect Kale's very name. "Maybe. So what?" she retorted, raising her chin defiantly.

Oren's lips curled and a new fierceness sparked in his eyes. "You spent the whole day with that monster. I gave you a day to indulge in your ridiculous need for adventure, and you're still not done?"

"You 'gave' me a day? How very generous of you," she sarcastically replied with a wrinkle of her nose. "And how did you know how long I was with him? Were you spying on me?"

"I had to know what you were up to."

Nahtaia briefly squeezed her eyes shut. "But you didn't report me," she said, trying to soothe her temper.

He paused for a moment, eyeing her, and she glared right back.

"I have my reasons," he said. "Reasons you clearly wouldn't understand."

Leaning on the fallen table behind her, Nahtaia raised her eyebrows in expectation. "Really? Like?"

His gaze remained on hers and that heaviness filled the air again. Oren's swallow was audible in the quietness, as was the croaking of the frogs' evening song. He was looking at Nahtaia in such a way that a sudden discomfort overcame her; a nervousness of sorts that created a strange, twisting sense in her belly. Something similar to what she felt with Kale.

"Well?" she said, mentally kicking herself when her voice cracked.

"You act like you don't know me, Nahtaia. You know how I feel about you."

Nahtaia clenched her teeth. Every so often, Oren would claim to hold affection for her. But she didn't believe him for a moment.

"As a matter of fact, Oren, I know you too well," she snipped in reply. "I know your tricks." She stepped toward him. "And I know you've got something up your sleeve."

"I don't have sleeves," Oren replied with a shake of his head. "I'm not tricking you. This is a serious matter.

You've lost your senses with this human, and I don't want you getting hurt. I *do* care about you."

Nahtaia huffed. Her blood grew hot and her ears were warm. "How sweet. You care so much that you're willing to risk *my* freedom." She shoved him back, only slightly budging him.

"Nahtaia, don't," Oren replied, frustration in his tone.

She stepped forward to shove him once more, but he snapped up her hands with his. "I asked you to stop!" he exploded. "You're such a pain! I am trying to *help* you, and you have made some kind of commitment to yourself to be difficult."

Nahtaia tried to pull away, but Oren held fast, so she gathered all the strength she had and slammed her shoulder into his chest.

In the blink of an eye, she was spun around, with her cheek against the tabletop. Oren's lips were by her ear as he said, "Bluebird, I know it's hard for you to accept, but I am going to be part of your life from now on. What I say, goes. And as you can see, the more you resist, the more you embarrass yourself."

She shoved against him and he released her.

"You'll learn to love me, if only for your own good," he replied, hovering near the door. "I'll see you tomorrow."

Oren shut the door behind him and Nahtaia growled. "I'll get you for this!"

"I'm looking forward to it!" he called from outside.

The first thought that came to Nahtaia's mind before going to sleep was how she would get away in the morning. It hadn't been too difficult the previous morning, so it shouldn't be too difficult the second time.

Early the next morning, Nahtaia cleverly used a distraction and a bird call to get out and back to the human farm. It took half the time her escape had the day before.

"Honestly," she muttered to herself, "how daft can some people really be?"

The morning was cool and the farm was only dimly lit by the slowly rising sun, but Kale wasn't difficult to spot. He stood in the same place where they had met the day before; he seemed to be waiting for her. He was ready with a coat and his tools and smiled widely as she emerged from the woods.

"Good morning," he greeted with a bow of his head.

"Good morning," Nahtaia replied with a mirroring smile.

He offered his elbow and they made their way to his workplace once again. The day was spent much like the previous one, discussing work and life, likes and dislikes. Again time passed quickly, the evening was shared with Terry, and then Nahtaia returned home.

Suspicions arose in Nahtaia when she found that Oren still had not reported her for leaving. But to her disappointment, security rose as well. For three days she couldn't escape Lyra, and she longed to watch Kale work, to have someone to talk to the way she could with him and Terry. She felt alone. At least Oren stopped hounding her so much. He had actually stopped speaking to her since the argument in her home.

On the fourth day, the two sentries watching Nahtaia's home finally let down their guard, withdrawing into conversation. The moment they both had their backs turned, Nahtaia fled toward Kale's workplace. He wasn't there.

She made her way to his home and was greeted by Grandmama.

"Darling, it's been a few days," she said with a crease between her brows. "Is everything all right?"

"Yes, I've just been busy around the house," Nahtaia replied. She wasn't lying. She was busy ignoring the guards...while in her home.

"Come in, come in. Terry and Kale have gone into town. They should be returning shortly." Grandmama led her to the kitchen, where she gestured for her to sit. "Tea?" she asked.

Nahtaia nodded, oddly comfortable alone with the elderly human.

"You haven't by any chance seen Willy about, have you?" Grandmama asked. "He left early this morning and I haven't seen him since. He's been acting strangely for days. Waking early. Coming home late in the day."

Nahtaia shook her head. Just then there was a scratching at the window, and the two turned their gaze toward the sound. When nothing more happened,

Grandmama stood with her hands on her hips and her lips pursed.

"Vile faeries," she grumbled, then turned back to the teapot over the fire.

Nahtaia's eyes widened in shock, offended by the haughty remark. The sweet, kind-hearted woman said the one thing she never imagined her to say. Nahtaia's tongue responded on impulse and was too quick.

"Pardon me?" she snapped. "How do you know it was faeries?"

Grandmama turned and frowned. "I've seen them, dear. They're always meddling about the farm."

A blush rose to Nahtaia's cheeks. Was she talking about her? Had she been seen in her faery form? All this time, she'd taken pride in her stealth!

With the cup of tea set before her on the table, all she could think about was leaving. She knew humans didn't like faeries, but she thought Terry and Kale's family was different. Now that she'd heard such negativity from Grandmama—the one whom Nahtaia suspected was the most kind-hearted to all creatures—her feelings were heavily changed.

"You don't see faeries at your home?" Grandmama went on, taking a seat at the table. "I think they have a town just within these woods. I'd be surprised if anyone didn't know about that. They're always flying about, making my animals nervous. Do you have any idea how difficult it is to milk a nervous cow?"

"I see faeries every day," Nahtaia blurted. "But they mind their own business." *For the most part*, she thought. "There is no reason for me to dislike them. It's humans that have always been the problem."

Grandmama raised her eyebrows in surprise. "You are something," she chuckled. "Never have I heard of a person taking up the side of a faery."

Nahtaia looked down at her hands. She must have seemed suspicious and knew that she had to get out. It would be the safest thing to do.

"Tell me," Grandmama went on, "why do you say that? Why would humans be the problem?"

Not wanting to push her luck any longer, Nahtaia rose from her seat and flashed a smile.

"It's just the inner musings of a young lady," she said. "Not to be taken seriously." She turned and started toward the door. "I've forgotten something back home. Thank you for the tea. I pray you have a good day."

"But you haven't even touched your cup," Grandmama frowned, now even more confused with the girl.

"I'm very sorry," Nahtaia called over her shoulder then muttered to herself, "You can keep your tea. Probably poisoned it anyway." How dare she think so low of faeries? It was humans who started the problems between them. It was humans who threatened the home of her kind, humans who killed her parents, and to top it off, faeries had been around for centuries longer than man.

When Nahtaia reached the line of trees at the edge of the forest, she looked back at the home. She suspected she wouldn't visit any longer. If sweet old Grandmama was so cold toward the fae, why would Kale and Terry be any different? They would never accept her if they were to find out the truth about her.

She thought back on a pair of humans she had met just before meeting this family; just before Minister Moriel called her in for distorting into a dog. They weren't hateful towards the fae. They actually found them fascinating and tried to make amends between species. But of course, they were only two of the innumerable humans of the world, and two couldn't change what happened in the past.

After turning back into her natural self, Nahtaia took a seat in the shrub she always sat in and looked at the farm. She was angry. Disappointed. The Mason family seemed like such good people and they were always so easy to talk to. It would be quite a journey to find faeries who were anything like them.

As she looked on in utter disappointment, something shook a shrub behind her. It was still too early in the day to be an owl and small animals were still scurrying about, so could be no predator nearby.

Oren, she thought with a roll of her eyes. No other faeries traveled that close to the farms. She didn't want to give Oren the satisfaction of turning around to look at him. It was when a twig snapped that she knew it couldn't be a faery. Just as she turned, a continuous wall of glass suddenly surrounded her, and on the other side was evil Willeim Mason.

It took Nahtaia a moment to realize what had happened before she fell into a panic. "No, no!" She gasped as Willeim twisted a top full of tiny air-holes onto the jar. "Willy! Willy, please!"

He started making his way toward his home, going around to the door at the back of the house. Nahtaia tried to distort herself but nothing happened.

"What?" she squeaked, then tried to work magic on the jar. Still nothing. She didn't understand. "Willy!" she cried. "Please, let me go!" He brought the jar to eye level and sneered. "I knew you were a faery. I knew it. No one believed me."

"Willy, you open this jar and let me out right this instant!"

"Do you know how hard it is when your family looks down on you? When they think you're imagining things? When they think of you as nothing but a child!"

He opened the door and snuck into his room.

"Grandmama won't be happy when she finds out about you," he went on. "She doesn't like faeries. But I have to wait until Kale and Terry come back, then they'll all see, or else Grandmama might grind you up first."

Blood drained from Nahtaia's face and she grew faint. He set the jar on a wooden table beside his bed. "I can hardly wait to see their faces," he sighed.

Nahtaia stood with her hands on the glass, still at a loss as to why her magic would not work.

"Listen to me, you little twit! You will open this jar and let me go!"

Willy frowned. "You're a lot meaner as a faery." After a short pause to study every part of her through the thick glass, he went on. "Kale won't be here for a while, and I'm hungry. I've been outside, waiting for you every morning for days. I almost lost hope." With a deep breath, he left the room, closing the door behind him, leaving Nahtaia in the strange, unfriendly room alone.

Dropping to the glass floor, she looked at her hands. *What happened?* she thought. *Why can't I distort?*

"It's the glass," a muffled voice spoke from above, outside the jar. A voice most well-known.

Nahtaia startled, shaken by the unexpected visitor, then jumped to her feet. "Spying on me again?" she calmly replied.

Oren dropped before her from the top of the jar. He was dressed in an odd black cloak that covered his entire body, even his head. He pulled off the hood, through which only his eyes had been visible, revealing his rather proud grin. "You ought to be glad I was," he replied.

Nahtaia frowned and sat back down. "Spare me."

"You can't use your magic. Glass is a shield against magic of the fae."

Her gaze faltered. "I didn't know that," she admitted.

"Well, you've never been captured before now, have you?"

"I'll get out one way or another."

He laughed. "And if you don't? Do you know what use humans have for faeries?" He leaned against the glass wall. "They catch us in jars like the one you find yourself in, and they pluck off our wings. They grind them into a fine dust to put into concoctions for things like speed dust or perfume."

Nahtaia's wings twitched at the thought.

"Of course, we bleed to death because they don't *cut* them off," he continued. "No, they take our flesh with the root of the wings, leaving us with gaping holes in our backs. Sometimes, if you've got a strong back, they have to cut the muscle. It's a very painful, gruesome death." He paused for a moment, walking around to the other side of the jar while running his fingers along the cool glass.

"Why are you telling me this?" Nahtaia asked, trying to hide her discomfort.

He flew back to stand in front of her and caught her gaze. "Because I want you to appreciate what I do for you."

Nahtaia glared at him, uncertain of what to do. The murmur of conversation between Grandmama and Willy floated on the air with the scent of meat and vegetables. Dinner was ready. It was only a matter of time before Willy would return.

If what Oren said was true, she did not wish that fate upon any faery, especially not on herself. If it wasn't true, Nahtaia would only have more reason to hate him. In her mind, it was a win-win situation, except for the part where Oren would think himself appreciated.

"Well, Bluebird?" he said with a half-smile. The dimple in his cheek was apparent in the setting sun, and a colorful vision of jamming a stick into it played in Nahtaia's mind.

"Just get me out of here," she muttered with her eyes on the ground.

He clicked his tongue with a sigh. "I don't like the tone in your voice. Try again."

Nahtaia clenched her teeth and flared her nostrils. With a deep breath, she slowly raised her gaze and forced a small smile. "Please, Oren," she tried. "I would appreciate your help in getting me out of this jar."

Chapter 6

The room felt like a cold and silent abyss as Nahtaia waited for Oren. He said he had a tool for opening jars like the one she found herself trapped inside. She was antsy, waiting for his return.

Hoping for Oren? she thought. *This situation's gotten really bad, Nahtaia.* Who'd have thought it?

Relief washed over her at the first sight of his glow as he came in through the window, but was quickly dammed up again when she heard Willeim's harsh footsteps on the wooden floors. Oren heard them as well and immediately dropped to the floor to extinguish his light and get lost in the shadows once again.

Nahtaia turned toward the door when Willeim entered the room and shut it behind him. He made his way to the jar and grinned a crooked grin when he saw she was still there.

"Willeim Mason!" she shouted, pounding on the glass. "You release me right now! Don't make me tell you again!"

He leaned down and his breath fogged the glass of the jar. "You're still here. Good. Wait until Terry and Kale see you. They'll have to believe me now."

Forget Oren, Nahtaia thought. Maybe she could manage to convince the little demon-boy to release her. "Willeim," she said as sweetly as she could. "If you release me, I will grant you three wishes." *Yeah. Right.*

His eyes brightened and his grin stretched. "Really?" he said, intrigued. "That's funny. I've never heard of anyone having their wishes granted by a faery."

Nahtaia tried to hold back her smile and nodded. "I can do it; it's my gift. I can change a bale of hay to a mountain of gold! If you let me go, that is. Then you won't ever have to see me and I'll leave your family alone."

Willeim's eyes fell to the desk as he mulled over the possibility, then he lifted his hand. Three wishes were awfully tempting for a boy his age, Nahtaia knew. He could have anything he wanted, but the moment he set his hand on the jar lid, she heard a familiar voice. It was Kale. Willeim jumped up, his gaze shifting between the door and Nahtaia. "Kale's here now," he whispered. "I've changed my mind. I'll show him first and then Grandmama and Terry."

"Willy," Nahtaia smiled, trying to seem as pleasant as she could. "Three wishes. Anything you can think of. Just don't let Kale see me."

He bit his lip and wrinkled his brow. "I can't think of anything I want more than for my family to believe me," he said, stepping closer to the door.

"I'll give you time!"

"And how do I know you won't run away? Grandmama says, 'never trust a faery.'"

Nahtaia grumbled, cursing the elderly woman under her breath as Willeim left the room to fetch his brother. She swirled around and looked for Oren in the shadows, but he was nowhere to be seen.

"Oren!" she called, pounding on the glass. "Oren! Hurry!"

Nothing.

"Where did you go?" she whispered with a whine. Horrid visions of her wings being plucked off her back by that wrinkled old hag played in her mind, making her face flush with anxiety. "Curse you, Oren! Where *are* you?"

The door clicked behind her and she turned to see the curious and flustered face of Kale.

Willy rushed to the jar on the table and snatched it, raising it up toward his brother. Nahtaia fell on her bottom at the sudden movement and braced her hands and feet against the glass to gain some stability.

"See?" he squealed. "I *told* you she's a faery!"

Kale was rooted to the ground, his brown hair falling gently before his blue eyes. At his brother's response,

Willy stepped forward and shoved the jar into Kale's stomach. Kale took hold of it, raising it to better see its contents.

"Now you know," Willy smirked. "Now you know I didn't lie to you. Now you have to tell me you're sorry."

"Willy," Nahtaia snapped, turning to the small child. "You are so proud of yourself, aren't you?"

"Of course I am!" he laughed. "I'm never right! No one ever listens to me!"

"Nahtaia?" Kale finally spoke, catching her attention. "Is it really you?"

She looked up with a frown. Was he against the fae like his grandmother? Would he be willing to strip her wings after all the time they spent together? And where was Oren?

"Kale," she started, unsure of what she was going to say. "I—"

"I should have known," he continued. His eyes remained focused on her, but something else glimmered in his gaze. Something that looked like pain. "Coming and going through the woods," he sighed. "You're a faery. Of course you are."

"Let me go, Kale," she tried. If Willeim wouldn't listen, maybe his brother would. "Please. I never meant to hurt anyone."

She'd never felt so frightened, but her life was in the hands of these humans and her magic would not work within the glass. Kale didn't respond but studied every inch of her. "Blue hair, blue lips, silver skin. The color is all wrong but the facial structure and voice is all you, no doubt."

Nahtaia didn't like the attention; it made her feel like a "plaything," as Oren had once put it.

"Don't let her go," Willy cut in. "We have to show Terry and Grandmama."

"Willeim Mason!" Grandmama called from the other room. "You come here this instant and clean up this mess!"

Kale's focus didn't waver when his brother let out a long sigh and started walking back to the kitchen.

"*Don't* let her out," he said over his shoulder.

"Kale," Nahtaia repeated as anger rose within her at his dissecting gaze. "Kale, just let me go."

Her voice shook with her plea, as much as she tried to steady it. She wouldn't show her fear. The more his attention shifted from her hair to her feet to her body, the more she forgot the days that had passed. They meant nothing to her any longer. Kale was just as horrible as his little brother for keeping her bottled up.

Her eyes brightened when he took hold of the jar's cap, partially opened it with a twist, then shook his head.

"I can't believe you didn't say anything," he quietly said. "I was hoping that we—" He stopped and sighed. "How foolish of me."

Nahtaia rose to her feet and braced herself against the glass in case he moved it again.

"I'm sorry," she said. "But I was afraid."

Kale frowned. "Afraid of what?"

Something moved behind Kale's shoulder and Nahtaia saw Oren, raising his bow and arrow to the back of Kale's neck. She noticed the yellow liquid on the tip of the arrow and gasped.

Poison.

"Oren, no!" she cried. Startled, Kale swung around and lost his grip of the jar. Nahtaia's stomach lunged into her throat as the jar dropped and she knocked her head on the side of the glass with a hiss. The jar toppled to the floor and the top popped off. She scrambled out and looked up at the men.

Oren pulled back the arrow, but before he could release it, she reached out to Kale and magic emanated from her hands. She didn't know what exactly she meant to do, but before she could work it out, Kale was on the floor beside her—five inches tall.

She stared at him wide-eyed and felt the blood drain from her face. He did the same. "Oh no," she squeaked.

"You-I-I'm," Kale couldn't get hold of his words as he looked down and around, confused with the sudden change of view. Willy's desk towered above them like a peakless mountain.

"In the name of the fae and all that's good and pure in this world, Nahtaia!" Oren shouted, landing beside her and Kale, his arrow still pointed at the human. "What have you done?"

Kale's chest rose and fell heavily with each breath as realization formed in his mind. "You-I-um-we…" His way with words was not getting any better. "Y-You shrank me! You-you *shrank* me! I'm miniscule! Why? Why did you do this?"

"Wait!" she cried, pressing her temples. "It's all right. I can fix this. Give me a moment." She closed her eyes and took a deep breath, readying her mind for another round of magic. With her hands reaching out toward Kale, she let out a breath and opened her eyes, feeling for the magic to leave her.

Nothing happened. She swallowed hard, and in the silence, everyone heard her.

Oren threw back his head. "Unbelievable!"

"Just wait!" she spat, then tried again. The stress coming from the men was not helping her straighten out her thoughts. Nahtaia yelped when something suddenly pinched her in the back. Her wings curled and disappeared with a poof of light.

"What was that?" she asked, unaware of what had happened.

Oren's jaw dropped and his eyes bugged from his head like a fruit fly. Kale's eyebrows rose with astonishment.

"What?" she asked as fear crept up her spine.

"Your wings," Oren said, his voice small and weak. "Your wings are gone."

"What?" She looked over her shoulder and shrieked.

"You've been humbled," he explained. He lowered his arrow and put a hand to his head.

Nahtaia lost her wits and spun in a panic, as if her wings would reappear if she looked hard enough.

"No, no, no, no!" she whimpered.

"Nahtaia, you have to turn me back," Kale cut in, reminding her of the other problem on her shoulders.

"But…my wings!"

"She can't turn you back," Oren growled. "Her magic is gone."

"What?" Nahtaia snapped to attention. "No. It's not gone. I'm just overstressed. I have to get my mind in order, then I can do—"

"You've been humbled, Nahtaia!" Oren shouted. He pointed a finger at Kale. "Because of *him*. Because of what you've done. Because you've stepped over the line, the Voices have taken your magic and your wings." His nostrils flared but his gaze softened in defeat. "You've been humbled."

Was it true? Was it possible? She'd never heard of such a thing. The Voices were supposed to be kind, not to mention too busy to regard any single individual. No, no it couldn't be true.

"Why would the Voices notice me?" she whispered. Sadness filled her as she searched herself but found no trace of magic. Even her silver skin lost its sheen.

Oren scoffed. "After all the foolish, unimaginable things you've done this moon alone, I wouldn't be surprised if they watched you on a regular basis for the fun of it!"

"Shouldn't we—" Kale started before Oren spoke over him.

"Fighting with rodents," Oren went on, counting on his fingers. "Distorting things that should not be touched. Oh, and I haven't forgotten the minotaur you charmed. Do you have any idea the trouble you caused for the ministers?"

Nahtaia pinched the bridge of her nose. "Oren, just stop. You see, this is why I can't stand you. You always have to remind me of my tiny mistakes—"

"And of course you think they were nothing," Oren snapped.

"They could be fixed!"

"Fix this!" Kale finally cried, stepping between the two faeries. "Fix *me*! Let's focus on the problem at hand. Forget what happened in the past! I'm standing here, five inches tall, with two faeries arguing about the Voices. There are other problems at the moment. Yesterday doesn't matter."

Nahtaia and Oren looked at Kale with narrowed eyes.

A silence fell between them before Nahtaia turned the accusations around. "This is your fault," she said.

Kale's jaw dropped. "My fault? I was just about to let you go!"

"If you'd have done it faster we wouldn't be in this mess!" she cried.

The voices of the three rose together in another band of arguments. Oren went on about Nahtaia's past mistakes. Nahtaia accused Kale of being insensitive and slow. Kale couldn't believe he was being blamed for anything. No one was getting anywhere.

"Kale?" a voice called from the kitchen. It was Grandmama.

Kale, Oren, and Nahtaia froze.

"I'll fetch him," Willy said.

When his footsteps vibrated through the floor, the three scattered to hide.

Willeim opened the door and froze. "Kale?" His eyes dropped to the floor and widened at the open jar. "No!" He frantically searched under the bed and desk, in the closet, out into the hallway. "Grandmama!" he finally cried, hurrying out of the room. "Grandmama! The faeries have Kale!"

After a moment, Willeim returned with Grandmama.

"And I caught her as a faery and she couldn't change and then I showed Kale and then you called me and now he's gone and Nahtaia isn't here either! See?" He picked up the jar. "She was in this jar!"

Grandmama stared at Willeim for a moment, then looked up at the window. "Child, if I find you're lying to me…"

"I'm not lying!"

She lowered onto the bed. "I've insulted the fae," she whispered. "This is my fault." She hesitated for another moment, then rose and hurried out of the house, shouting Kale's name with Willeim close behind.

"What am I supposed to do now?" Nahtaia scoffed, stepping back out into the open when it was clear.

Oren flung his bow over his shoulder and crossed his arms over his chest. "We go to the ministers," he said.

Nahtaia stiffened and shot a piercing glare at him. "Not the ministers. Moriel would drop me dead on the spot."

"Ministers?" Kale said.

"They are the only ones who can help," Oren insisted.

Nahtaia refused. The ministers were the last ones she'd turn to for help. She'd go to the Blacker Shadows on the other side of the world before sitting face to face with Moriel. The very idea of having those white eyes probe her innermost thoughts made her skin crawl. It would not happen. Not as long as she was alive and able to prevent it.

Oren hovered beside the window, deciding which way would be safer to leave. Kale's stare stayed on Nahtaia, likely still stunned that she'd kept such a secret from him. Nahtaia could feel his gaze and looked sidelong at him.

"What?" she snapped.

He shook his head and ran a hand through his hair. "I just still can't believe it."

Nahtaia crossed her arms and tapped a foot impatiently on the floor. "Which part? My being a faery or you being the size of a small cucumber?"

He didn't respond before Oren dropped down between them. "We go through the window," he said. "It'll be faster that way."

Kale nervously shifted his weight from foot to foot. "How, exactly?"

Oren laughed, throwing a passive glance at him. "Don't think for a moment that you're coming, human. Don't you think you've caused enough trouble?"

Nahtaia frowned. "Of course he's coming. I have to turn him back."

"Why?" Oren asked, eyeing the human from head to toe.

"Because I need to get my wings and magic back."

"And what does that have to do with him?"

Nahtaia impatiently curled her fists. "He may be needed and I will not risk losing him. Nor am I willing to return here to find him again later. Is that a suitable explanation or must we waste more time?"

Oren thought for a moment, then without another word, quickly snatched Kale by the arms and lifted him to the window sill.

Nahtaia gasped and cringed at Kale's disapproving shouts. When he was dropped onto the sill, he stepped back and stood against the window, his chest rising and falling with each nervous breath.

With a sigh of relief, Nahtaia looked around below the window as Oren flew back down to her.

"What are you looking for?" he asked. She didn't respond and he laughed. "I'm going to carry you up there," he said.

She shook her head. "No. You will not." With her chin stubbornly raised, she walked toward the white curtain that fell from above the window to the floor. She would climb it all the way up, and Oren would see that he wasn't needed.

Before she managed to even touch the material, Oren scooped her up into his arms.

"Hey!" she objected, kicking and pushing away from him as he flew unbearably slowly. "I said no!"

The corner of Oren's lips turned into a half-smile and he dropped his arm that had been holding Nahtaia's legs. With a scream, she held on to his neck, looking down at the drop that would surely break her legs. She turned her face up and grumbled at the pleased look on his face.

"I can get used to this, Bluebird," he said.

"This won't happen again," she replied, grunting as she struggled to hold on. "Now hurry up and put me down!"

Oren wrapped his arms around her waist, holding some of her weight, and laughed. When they finally reached the sill, Nahtaia rushed to the window and froze in stunned silence at what she saw. The drop from the window to the floor was a scary thought, but the length of the field toward the forest and then the distance from the edge of the trees to Lyra was utterly terrifying. Their journey seemed never-ending, and it hadn't even begun.

"Where do we intend on going?" Kale asked as they looked out onto the vast expanse of land.

"To Lyra," Oren said.

Nahtaia shook her head. "No. As long as Moriel is unaware of what's happened, I'm still safe. You can go to

Lyra," she said to Oren. "As for Kale and me, we're going to the Healing Pool."

Chapter 7

"You're joking, right?" Oren said, glaring at Nahtaia sidelong. "The Willow of D'Irdda, as close as it is, is not a reasonable goal in your condition, let alone the Healing Pool, which is even beyond the tree city."

Nahtaia stared out the window, her brow furrowed in annoyance. Of course that was his response. But she could see no other way.

Kale's stare jumped from her to Oren.

"How do you intend—" Oren continued before she cut him off.

"I will *find* a way," she quietly uttered. She looked up to Oren, whose expression only irritated her all the more. Brows cocked and lips pursed, he was giving her the "you have mental problems" look. How could he be so judgmental? "It's my only choice," she finally said.

"No, going to the ministers for help would be the better choice. What you're trying to do is suicide. It would take months to reach the Healing Pool without flying."

"There are other ways," Nahtaia snipped in response. When Oren cocked his brows as if waiting for a response, Nahtaia added, "Which I can't think of at this exact moment, but there *are* ways."

Kale finally spoke up. "We'll have to figure it out once we get away from here. We have to go now before my family returns. My grandmother is not fond of faeries, and she'll be quicker to stomp you than to think of asking your help."

"I could have told you that," Nahtaia muttered.

Air wafted in through the window, cool and refreshing compared to the stale and stuffy atmosphere of the home. It didn't seem that way when she'd visited the day before. Maybe it just felt like that now because of the stress.

"So I'll fly you to the tree line, just there," Oren said, gesturing toward the forest. He paused, watching Nahtaia, and she knew he waited for an argument from her.

Fortunately for him, she had no reason to argue. The distance was great, and she would flatten like a leaf if she dropped from the window.

Without another word, Oren took Nahtaia to the edge of the woods, then went back for Kale.

"Bring him back in one piece, or else," Nahtaia called to him as he flitted away. "Lousy toad." Her blood boiled when, a moment later, Oren returned holding Kale by one arm, his legs flailing aimlessly. When Oren dropped him on the grass, she helped Kale up. "Are you all right?" she asked him.

He stood, brushing grass and dirt from his clothes with a frown. "I'm fine," he said.

There was something different about Kale and it was difficult for Nahtaia to ignore. He didn't seem like the same kind-hearted man he'd been the previous week. He was distant and wouldn't look her in the eyes anymore. That bothered Nahtaia, but then another part of her told her it was fine—that she didn't care. He was just a human, after all.

Oren stepped between the two, straightening his back to make his full size more obvious beside Kale. "It's dangerous to stay here," he said.

Nahtaia took a deep breath and held it in for a moment. It was difficult not to call Oren out on his behavior. His jealousy toward the human was ridiculous.

"Which way is west?" Nahtaia asked, looking up at the sky. Kale and Oren both turned to her.

"You're a faery and you don't know which way is west?" Kale said.

Nahtaia pressed her lips in a tight line. "What does being a faery have to do with a sense of direction?"

Oren took Nahtaia's hand in his and pulled her along. "West is this way."

She dug her heels into the ground and jerked away. "I can walk just fine, you know!"

"I need to keep you beside me at all times, so you don't run off and do something stupid again," Oren replied. He grasped her hand again and kept walking.

Kale followed close behind, watching the two quarrel.

"Oren, I said stop!" she exclaimed.

Kale lunged forward and grabbed Oren's wrist, pulling it to loosen his grip on Nahtaia.

"Let her go," Kale said quietly.

At Kale's touch, Oren whipped around, letting go of Nahtaia but snatching the collar of Kale's shirt, holding him inches from his face. The motion was so swift, Nahtaia hardly knew what happened.

"Don't touch me, human," Oren said in a low growl. The tone of his voice alone was threatening.

Kale swallowed and was about to reply when Nahtaia shoved Oren.

"*You* don't touch *him*!" she demanded. "Why don't you just go home and let Kale and me fix this ourselves?"

"You need me," he replied. His eye contact with Kale was unfaltering, ensuring the human would feel inferior. "I can protect you."

Nahtaia pushed through them. "I don't need your protection."

Oren finally let go of Kale and laughed, turning his olive gaze to Nahtaia.

"Oh, right. I remember how well you handled the owl yesterday. You've got the survival skills of a wild cat, no doubt."

She turned west with a scowl, and Kale followed close behind.

Though the sun was still a couple hours above the horizon, the forest was full of shadows. Thankfully, the owls and other larger birds were still sleeping, but they would awaken to the nocturnal call of the moon. Small critters shuffled through shrubs and the canopy. The faeries were not alarmed by the sounds, but Kale didn't know any better and he jumped at every snap of a twig or shake of a limb.

Nahtaia hissed. "There is an absurd amount of sharp things on the ground," she whined.

Oren looked on with a grin. It was when she stopped to remove a thorn from her foot that he flitted past Kale and walked beside her.

"Enjoying your trip?" he joked.

Nahtaia peered up at him through her lashes, then stopped again with a cry. Another thorn.

"You think this is funny, do you?" she asked. "Go ahead and laugh. Moon fae have no use for shoes the way pine faeries do."

That caught Kale's attention. "Moon fae?" he asked.

Nahtaia turned and pursed her lips with a frown. "Yes." Her eyes hesitated between his curious gaze and the floor. "I'm a moon faery." She turned and continued on her way.

"What makes you a moon faery?" he asked, running until he reached her other side.

Oren groaned and rolled his eyes.

"My nature, my ability, and of course, the most obvious thing, my color," she replied, stepping over a tiny shard of broken glass—a remnant of a human traveler.

"Your nature?"

"By the Highest, can you be any more irritating?" Oren complained.

"Shut up, Oren," Nahtaia snapped, then looked back to Kale. "Yes. I like water and the night; moonlight, specifically. It comforts me."

"So blue is the color of all moon faeries?" Kale asked.

Nahtaia nodded in reply.

Oren laughed and put an arm around her shoulders. "But you should know, Nahtaia is not like every other moon faery, human." He grinned when she pushed him away. "She's fiery. Most lunar fae are deep and serious, able wielders of the greatest abilities. You know her power? She holds the greatest of it amongst the fae. Makes the rest of us look pathetic, but the ministers can't control her. Most of us answer to their law but she's got a talent for breaking it."

Kale didn't look too surprised. He turned his gaze and studied Oren. "And you? What kind are you?"

"He's a piner," Nahtaia answered with a grimace.

"A pine *faery*," he corrected. "We're the military hand of the species." A smug air surrounded him as he puffed up with pride and stroked his goatee. "We're security—protectors and fighters. Not to mention, the strongest and largest of them all."

"Spare me," Nahtaia mumbled and climbed over a large rock. "Oren is the irritating one of the species and is always around when you *don't* need him. He's got a talent for making bile rise up in my throat, and the ministers have him on a chain for their every beck and call. That's his nature in a nutshell."

Kale couldn't help laughing but suppressed it when Oren turned to him angrily.

"I'm sorry," he said, then looked back to Nahtaia, who winked in return. "But what do pines have to do with security?"

Oren jumped to answer the question before Nahtaia had a chance to put him down again. "We were originally the faeries cleaning up the ground after winter to make room for spring, but our alertness and courage shone through as we worked the grounds at the edge of Lyra. Eventually, they chose those of us with more girth and put us on security instead."

Nahtaia clutched her hands to her chest and let out a long exaggerated sigh. "Oh, Oren!" she cried." Your bravery is much too…brave for the forest floor! Here, have a sword and follow the cute little blue faery around to keep her from unruly behavior!" She nearly screamed the last word.

Oren rolled his eyes. "She just has no respect for all we do for our people."

Kale's face brightened with curiosity. "Is that what happened?" he asked. "You were told to follow Nahtaia?"

"To *protect* her," Oren corrected.

In the distance, Nahtaia spotted a bush full of berries and quickly made her way to it. "I told you. I don't need protection," she said as she plucked two from it and handed them to Kale, then helped herself before continuing on her way. "I've survived this long without you."

"Right, and without me, you'd still be trapped inside that jar."

"So," Kale cut in, his curiosity about faeries swelling, "what do you call your ability?"

"Distortion," she replied, taking a bite of the red berry, then wiping her mouth with the back of her hand. "I can change anything. Color, size, shape—whatever I want."

Kale looked up at Oren and glanced at the quiver slung over his back.

"I have good aim, great strength, and amazing speed," Oren said.

Nahtaia could swear his chest inflated to twice its size with his reply. "And a colossal ego that can make you sick," she added, then dropped to the floor with a groan. Taking her foot, she brushed off some dirt and pieces of leaves. In less than an hour, her dainty feet were blistered and bleeding. "I need shoes," she said with a pout. "I can't go on like this."

Oren leaped into the air and disappeared into the canopy. Nahtaia didn't give him a second glance but turned to Kale instead, who took a seat beside her.

"You don't walk much, I gather," he said.

"No," she replied. "Almost never."

Kale wrinkled his nose and let out a chuckle. "Were you always barefoot when you came to see me?"

Nahtaia laughed and nodded. "Yes, but magic gave me an illusion of shoes."

There was a pause in conversation and Kale looked up, scanning the woods. He cleared his throat and asked, "Why *did* you come to see me, Nahtaia?"

Nahtaia froze, not looking up from her feet. She didn't really know the whole answer to that. "Infatuation?" she replied, though it came across as more of a question. "Um," she lifted her gaze to his for a fleeting second. Before she could go on, Oren dropped back down beside her with a rolled-up leaf in his hand.

Kale looked down at the ground and started to draw in the dirt with his finger.

"Give me your foot," Oren said, sitting in front of Nahtaia.

"What? No." She frowned.

"Just—" He took her foot, crossing his legs around her ankle so she couldn't pull free. "Give it."

Her jaw dropped as she exchanged glances with Kale. He only shrugged in reply.

Oren unrolled the leaf and revealed a thick spread of honey-colored tree sap which he globbed onto her feet before smearing it with his hands.

"What are you—" she started, then laughed uncontrollably as he oozed the sap through her toes. "Stop! Stop it!" she giggled. The harder she tried to pull away her foot, the more he tightened his hold. Nahtaia laughed until she teared, and Kale couldn't help but laugh at the sight.

Oren took the leaf, pulled it apart in two halves, and wrapped her feet in it while Nahtaia wiped her face dry. "What is this for?" she asked.

"The sap will heal your blisters and make your feet soft. The leaves will let it do its work while you walk."

"Oh," she said, then studied his fancy handiwork. "Thank you." She looked up to find him gawking.

"What did you just say?" he asked.

Nahtaia frowned. "Oh, shut it, Oren. I can be nice when it's deserved."

Oren's smile only spread and he stood up. "I'm going to find somewhere safe for us to sleep tonight."

"It's not that late," she called after him, but he flew away so fast, he was already too far to have heard her.

Kale pulled his legs up and crossed them, then looked up to her. "Didn't Oren say the Healing Pool is a little too far?" he asked.

"I don't have a choice, Kale," she replied. "The Voice of Mae'Ehr is nice to faeries. The ministers will kill me if I return to Lyra."

Kale stiffened. "Kill you?"

"Banish, kill; it's the same to me." She stared at the ground and thought on what Moriel would have to say about her situation. He already made it clear that she had gone too far, and that was before she even met Kale and his family.

She tried to push the image of his pale eyes out of her mind and focused on a pebble at her feet. She formed an image in her mind and tried to mentally pull and mold the pebble into any desired form.

Nothing. She felt absolutely nothing. Her magic *was* gone and with that realization setting in, she felt her hope dwindle away.

Kale's hand reached out and took hers. "We'll fix this," he said reassuringly.

Nahtaia looked at him and squeezed his hand in return, taking notice of the callouses on his palms. She took his hand and turned it palm up, running her fingers over the tough skin. "You work hard," she said with a small smile.

"Since I was very young," he replied.

After a moment, Kale's other hand sandwiched hers and she nervously looked up at him through her dark lashes.

"Even now," he said, "knowing what you are, I still enjoyed the time we had together." He paused in thought. "If I could go back, I wouldn't have changed a thing."

Nahtaia knew he was trying to make her feel better but it was hard to ignore the emphasis he put on "what you are." He spoke as if she were some kind of animal.

A snap sounded behind her and she turned to find see Oren staring at Kale with a hatred she'd never seen on him. No, he wasn't looking at Kale; he was looking at their hands.

"What?" Nahtaia puffed, taking her hands away and crossing her arms.

"I found a place," he said through tight lips, his eyes moving up to meet Kale's.

Nahtaia jumped to her feet and walked past Oren, trying to ignore the sap oozing through her toes with every step. "Oh, goody," she said. "Let's go, then."

Kale stood and followed after her, but Oren stopped him, grabbing his upper arm.

"She's not human, boy," Oren said quietly enough so Nahtaia wouldn't hear.

Kale nodded. "I know."

Oren looked sidelong at the human, who was just taller than Nahtaia yet shorter than himself. "Just remember that." He released his hold on Kale and led the way to the shelter for the night.

Nahtaia let out a tired, even breath as she turned her ears slightly away from the men. Oren was not getting easier to deal with.

Chapter 8

Oren had found an abandoned rabbit den away from sight, but it was rather small and half buried by time and travelers. But by the time they arrived, it was dark and too late to find another form of shelter, so they were forced to deal with the tight space for the night.

Nahtaia walked in first and lay down, then, following a scuffle and harsh whispering, Oren lay down beside her—too close for her comfort. When she asked what the noise and whispering was about outside, they both shrugged.

The night passed with elbows in her side and snoring, though she couldn't tell which of the men was doing the snoring. It didn't matter anyway, and the moment the sun shone through the trees and the forest took on the soft, yellow glow of dawn, she shoved the men awake and prodded them out of the hole.

"I'm assuming you didn't sleep well," Oren said, rubbing the place in his back that was abused by her tiny but pointy finger. "I can't imagine why else you'd be so moody."

She didn't care to respond and continued through the forest, with Kale lagging behind. Oren was obviously not fond of having him around and kept Nahtaia busy with his own imposed conversation, to which she replied with silence.

The three travelers were sore and grumpy as the hours passed. Nahtaia tossed an occasional glance behind, making sure Kale was still there. Every time she would look, Oren would either turn himself with an intimidating scowl or put an arm around her, so as to put her attention back on him.

"If we just go to the right, we could spot Minister Sentinian's house in less than two hours," Oren said.

"I told you, I refuse to go to any ministers. If I can just get to the elves, I'm sure they could help me, and Lyra would never know anything happened," Nahtaia replied.

Clearly, Oren didn't like her response. He ran a hand over his jaw with a groan and said, "You don't think Lyra noticed our absence by now? It's been two days."

"Then go, Oren," she said, gesturing to the right.

"I'm not leaving," he started before noticing Kale in his peripheral vision. "What do you want?" he snapped.

Kale shrugged and stepped beside Nahtaia. "To help," he replied. "I'm still here, too, whether you like it or not."

Oren frowned as Kale offered his elbow to Nahtaia. She looked up at him with a half-smile, deciding not to share her pleasure in his ability to stand up to Oren.

"Why, thank you," she said, hooking onto his arm. From the corner of her eye, she saw Oren's hand find the wood of his bow.

"By the Highest Power, Oren, calm down!" Nahtaia snapped. "At least he thought to be helpful in the first place. All you've done is tell me everything I'm doing wrong."

"Right. I've done *nothing* helpful," Oren replied with a scoff. "You were barely walking yesterday, in case you forgot."

Nahtaia curled her toes in the drying sap around her feet and bit the inside of her cheeks. He wasn't wrong. He was the one who found them a place to sleep and who brought her and Kale something to eat more often than not. He was also the first one who took action to get her out of the jar.

Her gut twisted with guilt. "Ok. Fine. You're right. You *have* done some things that deserve recognition, and for that, I thank you. But when every good deed is followed by an argument between the only two people around me, things get frustrating."

Oren raised his eyebrows and blinked in surprise.

"What?" Nahtaia asked, crossing her arms over her chest. "Why are you looking at me like that?"

"I've never seen you open up. Especially to me," Oren replied.

Nahtaia wrinkled her nose in annoyance. "If you were kind more often, then you would hear it more often."

Oren pressed his lips in a tight line and glowered at Kale, who sniggered beside her. The human's face quickly turned bright red.

It took moments of dead silence between the three before another word was spoken.

"Who are you, anyway?" Kale said with a swallow. Nahtaia got the sense he was trying to ease tensions. Which was a foolish thing to try when it came to Oren. "I mean, how did you two meet?"

Nahtaia looked up at Oren with a frown. "He's been there for as long as I can remember. For as long as I've had my gift," she added. "Magic Discovery Lessons, Magic Use Lessons—"

"—lunch," Oren interrupted with a laugh.

"Oh, yes. That was the worst." She paused in thought for a moment before giggling. "Remember that time you nearly ate that bug?" Nahtaia asked Oren smugly.

"I didn't 'almost eat' it," Oren scoffed. "You jumped on my back and forced it into my mouth."

"What, like you couldn't fight me off?"

"I was off balance with wet wings—from you pushing me into the river. You know, almost every bad thing that's ever happened was because you were trying to get rid of me while I was just trying to keep you out of trouble."

Nahtaia's ears burned scarlet. Like she needed a babysitter! "No one asked you to keep me out of trouble. I've always been able to handle things myself."

The two went off on another tangent about who was at fault and who did worse things to the other, until Kale finally stepped between the pair.

"All right, all right, all right!" he said, separating them. "Are you two always like this?"

They glared at one another, then Nahtaia turned away, stubbornly crossing her arms. Kale looked to Oren, who cocked a brow with a sigh.

"*She's* always like this," Oren said. "She was even worse before…" he paused, passing a fleeting glance to Nahtaia. "Before her *flowering,* if you know what I mean."

Nahtaia whipped back at him. "Excuse me! Who do you think you are?"

"Never mind! Calm down!" Kale groaned. "Never in my life have I seen any two people more childish than you two. And I thought Terry and Willy were bad."

Nahtaia shook her head in disbelief, then stomped off ahead while Oren smiled at Kale with a wink. "At least I got her off your arm."

The sappy leaves that Oren wrapped around Nahtaia's feet were torn before the end of the day. While he was off looking for another den or shelter for the night, she peeled away the remains as Kale looked on. The sap was hard and crusted, tickling her with every attempt to remove it, but they did what Oren claimed they would. Her cuts were already healing and the pain was gone, for the most part.

The air was still and the sounds of birds startled the pair with every chirp or caw. Shadows spread over the gray outstretched fingers of the trees that played with the eyes of the small people on the ground. Nahtaia found herself secretly hoping for Oren to hurry and return. After all, he was the one with the weapons.

"What do you intend on telling the Voices—assuming you do find them?" Kale asked, leaning back onto his elbows.

"I'm not sure," she replied, her eyes on her feet as she avoided his gaze. Inwardly, she was thankful for the crusty yellow sap. It was a welcome distraction from the awkward feelings that came from their conversations since the shrinking incident. "I'll decide when we get closer."

He nodded and looked up into the treetops. An owl hooted and Nahtaia quickly peered into the branches as well.

"We should get going," she whispered. "It's going to be dark soon and we still don't have anywhere to sleep."

Standing up beside her, Kale searched the trees. "Shouldn't we wait for Oren?"

"He'll find us."

Flapping wings sounded from above and Nahtaia took Kale's hand, pulling him along faster while calling for Oren. "Where are you?" she whined.

In the distance was a thorny bush—the best thing next to shelter for them. If they stayed near the center, they'd be all right until Oren returned to take them somewhere better.

Nahtaia pointed to the shrub and hurried toward it. They carefully climbed a few branches up, dodging the many thorns, and settled near the middle of the plant. Another hoot sounded.

"Okay, so owls are not good for us," Kale said, sitting on a branch just above the one Nahtaia sat on. "Which is odd, as they're a good thing for us farmers."

She shook her head and tried to relax. The stress of the situation made it difficult for her to focus, and Kale's almost constant chattering made it even worse.

"What else should we be watching out for?" Kale went on. He obviously wanted to keep her talking, for whatever reason.

"Hawks, crows, snakes." Nahtaia sighed. "Anything that eats meat."

"All right," he replied. After a moment, he stepped down onto her branch and sat beside her. Nahtaia frowned and scooted closer to the stalk of the plant to make more room for him—and to give herself more personal space. There was a strange emotion coming from him, and it made her uncomfortable. Since she was back to her normal size, it was difficult to remember him as the Kale she knew just days before. The way he'd left her cooped up in that jar while he scrutinized her left her feeling leery of him.

"Nahtaia," he said, staring again.

Her skin pricked at the tone of his voice. *Here comes another talk,* she thought.

"While Oren is gone, I want to talk. I mean," he took a deep breath, "I just want to know."

Nahtaia leaned as far toward the stalk as physically possible while he spoke.

"I want to know what was going on in your mind when you came to my workplace. I mean, why did you come?" he asked as he fiddled with his fingers. "Not that I didn't enjoy your company. I did—I really did, but I just want to know if you, maybe..." he paused and wiped his brow that suddenly glistened with sweat. Nahtaia hesitantly looked up at him from the corner of her eye, wondering why he stopped and praying desperately that he wouldn't go on. He was still watching her, and then he did the last thing she ever expected from anyone—especially a human. He leaned in and pressed his lips against hers.

Nahtaia froze, unsure of how to accept the flutters that exploded in her belly. She didn't kiss back and she didn't pull back; she just froze until he pulled away. Her mind was surprisingly calm—foggy, as if storm clouds covered her consciousness, veiling her ability to react. She stared at him for a moment, then climbed down from the shrub.

"Nahtaia?" He climbed down after her, but she walked on. "Nahtaia, w-what is it?" He hurried to her side, but she kept her eyes on the way before them. When she wouldn't respond, he stepped in front of her, stopping her. "Say something."

She swallowed hard and avoided eye contact. "I-I don't know what that was."

"It was a kiss," he said, taking her hand.

She shook her head. "I know it was a kiss, but I don't know what you're trying to say," she explained, then stepped around him.

"I'm trying to say I like you, Nahtaia."

Finally she did something. She laughed. One quick *ha*.

"Did you just scoff at me?" He frowned. "I do like you. I like you very much and I think you like me, too, or else you wouldn't have come back so many times to see me."

"You're human, Kale," Nahtaia said, now feeling slightly rattled.

He remained in step with her, trying to catch her attention. "And that's important?"

She wrinkled her brow and gave him a fleeting glance. "Yes, you're human and I'm a faery. We can't possibly—"

"What does that have to do with anything? We're still people. Elves and humans get along fine," Kale said.

"There's one thing elves have that faeries do not—height."

"But your ability is distortion. We're the same size now and we've been the same size every time we were together."

When Nahtaia didn't respond, he stopped her again. "Listen, I just want to know this, then. Why did you come to see me if you didn't like me?"

Nahtaia licked her lips that were suddenly dry as bark, still unable to meet his gaze. How could she explain herself to him when she couldn't sort through her emotions for herself? "I do like you, but I just don't know what, exactly, I'm feeling about—"

Before she finished, Kale took her face in his hands and kissed her again. Nahtaia held her breath and tensed. The already sore muscles in her legs twitched, and she started feeling dizzy. She pushed a hand against Kale's chest and stepped back.

"Stop it," she said. "Please. I don't know what—"

"So you punch me, and you kiss the human," Oren's voice spoke from behind her. She whipped around and felt even more dizzy as a flood of blood rushed to her face.

"I didn't kiss him," she said. "He kissed me!" Why she felt the need to explain herself to him, she didn't know, but she immediately regretted it.

Oren reached into his quiver, snatching an arrow, then stalked toward Kale. "I told you to watch yourself!"

"Oren!" Nahtaia cried, stepping in his way. She took hold of the arrow and tried to take it from him, but she wasn't strong enough. "What do you think you're doing?" His eyes were focused on Kale like a predator on its prey and Nahtaia stood on her toes, trying to steal his gaze. "Why should you care what Kale does?"

"The boy needs to keep to his own species," Oren snapped.

Kale stepped forward. "I think she's capable of making her own decisions."

Before Oren could step forward again, Nahtaia shoved against him. "It doesn't matter to *you* anyway, so let me deal with it."

That got his attention and he looked down at Nahtaia. Words hung on his lips, but he didn't speak them.

"Oren," she sighed, glad he was calm enough to listen. "I need Kale to get things back to normal. Let it go." She stared at him until he finally loosened his hold on the arrow, then she stepped around him with a huff, continuing on her way.

Nahtaia was angrier than she'd ever been in her life. Angry at Kale for kissing her and making her feel guilty. Angry at Oren for pretending to care about her. Angry at herself for being such a dunce as to get them into this situation in the first place.

Oren looked back at Kale, who stared after her.

"If you touch her one more time," Oren started.

"She wouldn't let you do anything," Kale replied.

Nahtaia turned around. "You two better not still be talking. There are birds and it is getting dark and I would rather not have to deal with any more problems now. Oren, where are we staying tonight?"

He turned and started toward her with a cocky swagger to his walk before pointing to the treetops. "A squirrel's den. Up there."

Nahtaia threw her hands into the air with a groan. "Great."

When she started toward the tree, Oren turned back to Kale with a grin. "She needs us, but you both need me," he said.

Kale frowned and followed after Nahtaia, who reached the tree first. When both men joined her, she looked to Oren. "Take him gently," she said.

With a half-smile, Oren grabbed Kale by the back of the shirt and jumped into the air. After dropping him on the branch sticking out from the den entrance, he winked and went back for Nahtaia. Landing in front of her, he crossed his arms and smiled. "Ready?" he asked.

Nahtaia looked up at the tree and saw Kale watching them.

"Well?" Oren pressed.

"Okay, just—" she paused, then took a step toward him. "How do we—"

Oren opened his arms wide and grinned. "Climb aboard."

"What?"

He laughed when she took a step back. Of course, he had to make the situation more awkward than necessary. He couldn't just grab her like he grabbed Kale. He was going to make *her* go to *him*.

"Come on," Oren said. "We don't have all night."

Teeth and fists clenched, Nahtaia stepped forward and wrapped her arms around his neck. "Let's get this over with."

He looked down at her with his dimpled smile, clearly enjoying the situation. She let out a squeak of disapproval when he snaked his arms around her waist and jerked her closer.

"For safety," he said.

"Oren, shut up and make this fast."

With a light flutter of his wings, the two rose slowly above the ground.

"This is not funny, Oren," she snapped. She knew he was going slowly on purpose.

"What, exactly, do you like about that human?" he asked. Though his tone sounded entertained, there was a hint of restraint.

She bit her lip. "I do not need to explain myself to you," she replied, suddenly noticing the strong woodsy scent that came from Oren's hair. Or breath. She couldn't tell.

"I'm curious. I've never heard of a faery being attracted to a human."

"I'm not attra—"

"Is it the hair? Do you like short hair better? Or is it the smell? He smells something like rotting onion, in my opinion, but if that's what you like, more power to you, you know?"

"Please, just—"

"Or maybe just the idea that he's not a faery. You do seem to have an aversion to your own kind." His tone started getting rougher. "I mean, a faery can say or do exactly what you'd want him to, but you'd still hate him in the end."

Nahtaia started wriggling, trying to free herself from him, but he just held on tighter. At least he flew faster to set her down. She shoved him away and stomped past Kale into the den.

"She's a handful," Kale said.

"You've no idea."

The two looked at each other, then started in after her. When Kale began moving faster, Oren pushed him, knocking him down onto the branch, calling over his shoulder, "Remember what I said about touching her."

The night passed much quicker and more comfortably compared to the previous one—for the men. Nahtaia had space enough to her liking, yet she couldn't find the peace of mind that would allow her to rest. Her mind was actively sorting through the events of the past two days. Kale's declaration of feelings for her, Oren's threatening disposition toward Kale, and, of course, her lack of understanding concerning her own emotions.

When it came to Kale, she was just confused. Something inside her that told her she did like him. He was attractive, for a human, but at the same time, he wasn't very brave; not as adventurous as she'd hoped.

He did have his good side, though: his kindness. His softness. His way with words and skills she'd never seen in a faery. He made his feelings clear, unlike faery men who expected a girl to read their minds.

Enough about Kale, she thought, sitting up. As the men slept, they seemed so innocent. Well, Kale, at least. Nahtaia knew better when it came to Oren.

She rose from the leaves and moss she'd piled up for herself to sleep on and stepped out onto the branch extending from the entrance to the den. There was no sign of predators, but she still made sure not to wander far. Spotting a sliver of moonlight that broke through the trees, she sat down in it, wrapping her arms around herself against the night chill. She turned her face up toward the stream of light and closed her eyes, waiting for her skin to absorb the pale magic, but she felt nothing. Whereas her skin would usually ripple with pleasure and warm comfort from moonlight, she found herself feeling empty and cast aside.

Tears welled in her eyes, but she blinked them back before they fell down her cheeks. She would regain her magic. She had to.

"You still glow," Oren's voice came from behind her.

Nahtaia huffed and grit her teeth until her jaw ached. "Of course, even in the middle of the night you come to torment me," she replied.

He raised his hands in surrender and smiled. "No, no tormenting. I come peacefully."

Nahtaia narrowed her eyes. "Why aren't you sleeping?" she asked as he took a seat beside her. She tensed when his leg brushed against hers.

"I've been trained well to wake up at any sign of distress," he said.

"There was no sign of distress."

He laughed and leaned back onto his hands, swinging his feet over the edge of the branch. "No offense, but you are the sign of distress. You may as well change your name to Distress."

Nahtaia sighed, exhausted of his jokes. "All is well. You can go back to bed." She could feel his eyes on her, but he didn't say anything for nearly two minutes.

"You still glow," he repeated. "Do you know what that means? All hope is not lost. There still is some magic in you."

The pair heard Kale shifting around, but he quickly grew quiet again, assuring them he was still asleep. Nahtaia put her face back up to the moon and was startled when Oren touched her hand. He was warm and his skin was soft. Immediately, she remembered the callouses on Kale's hand. Slowly Nahtaia sat up and took Oren's hand, turning it over. His were much larger but nearly callous free. For the fae, it had nothing to do with how much physical work one's life consisted of. They just had stronger skin.

"What?" Oren asked. "Not quite like the human's, is it?" Disgust was clear in his voice.

She dropped his hand and turned from him. "You have to make everything about you, don't you?"

"I just want to understand."

"There's nothing more to say. I never intended for any of this to happen. If I hadn't been so foolish to use magic without a clear idea of what I wanted to happen, I would have left that farm and never returned. But no, instead, you had to appear, more than glad to kill him."

"To save you," Oren scoffed.

"Please."

Oren rubbed his eyes, flustered with frustration. "Nahtaia, you just can't accept anyone's help." He stood up and ran his hands through his hair. "You know, one day, you'll be all alone and you'll be the one at fault." He got up and started back toward the den.

She thought about that and felt an overwhelming sadness wash over her. He was right. Maybe that was the real reason she didn't have anyone. She blamed it on Oren for interfering in her every conversation with a man, but maybe it was just *her*. After all, she enjoyed Kale's company and admitted that it felt good to know he liked her, yet she couldn't bring herself to show her feelings for him. If she had any. Did she? She couldn't really decide. Either way, she didn't have anyone to call her own while every other faery in Lyra did.

Nahtaia looked down at her hands and said, "No, Oren, I *am* alone."

He stopped and frowned before responding, "*I'm* still here," then he made his way inside.

Chapter 9

It was midday, dark, and humid as the trio continued their way through the woods. The faeries sensed the rains coming in the morning and decided to try to cover some distance before having to find another shelter. While Kale followed close behind Nahtaia, Oren lagged behind.

Thunder rolled in the distance, and another hour later, began to vibrate through the ground. Kale looked up through the canopy and jumped as Oren flew just above his head, disappearing through the leaves. Seeing the opportunity, he hurried beside Nahtaia.

"Is everything all right?" he asked.

Nahtaia threw a quick glance up at him with a small smile. "Sure," she replied.

"You two are awfully quiet today."

As she shrugged, her foot caught on a tree root, causing her to stumble, but Kale caught her arm just before she hit the ground. She muttered a quiet "Thank you" and continued on.

"I'm sorry," he sighed. "For kissing you. I thought that maybe if you'd see that I felt something for you, you'd open up to me."

Nahtaia stopped and turned around. "I'm not mad at you," she said. "I simply want to get everything back to normal and go home." She turned back, climbed over a fallen branch and added, "I'm in too much trouble to think about kisses. I just want my magic back."

Kale frowned. "What is so great about magic?"

Nahtaia chuckled and arched a brow. "Go cut off an arm and then ask me that question. Faeries are born with magic. We *are* magic."

"What happens when you get it back? What then?"

"Then you go back to your farm and she comes home with me," Oren's voice cut in behind them. They both stopped and turned with identical frowns.

"Not 'with you,' Oren. But yes, I would like to go home," Nahtaia said and walked away.

Kale followed after her.

"Boy," Oren hissed, "you don't understand, do you? You have no place with her. She and I—we are of the fae. We are allied with magic and the mystical. And you are just human. End of history lesson."

"Will you two stop jabbering," Nahtaia called from ahead. "It's going to start raining any moment now."

Kale looked up and Oren flew to Nahtaia. Thunder clapped and another sound came from deeper within the woods—hoof beats. The three stopped and looked off into the direction from which the sound came. Oren grabbed

Nahtaia's wrist and pulled her to the shelter of a small bush. Kale joined them.

"What is it?" he asked. The only reply was Oren and Nahtaia holding their noses. They looked at one another with creased brows and said, "Minotaurs."

Kale took a deep breath and shook his head. "I smell nothing."

"Of course you don't," Oren mumbled. "Over time you get used to even your own bad smell."

"Oren," Nahtaia snipped before recoiling closer to him at the sight of one of the large creatures. "Oh boy," she said with a swallow.

Two giants, eight feet tall and nearly four feet wide, stalked through the woods. Their backs were hunched with the weight of bulging muscles and three-foot-long curved horns. In their hands were enormous double-headed axes. One hoof alone spanned double the length of the three faeries stretching arm to arm in a line.

"Don't tell me," Oren whispered. "That's the one, isn't it?"

Nahtaia said nothing as the bull-headed creatures stamped passed them.

"'The one?'" Kale whispered.

Oren couldn't help himself. "The story is quite unusual and seems even more far-fetched when seeing the size of the minotaurs here. One would think, how could such a small faery do any harm to such an enormous creature? Right? Well, little Nahtaia here charmed one of those two." Oren chuckled.

"The smaller of the two," she added.

"There's a smaller one?" Oren replied, looking on. "They look equally monstrous."

Kale's eyes widened in surprise. "Charmed? You really charm things? Like in the song?"

The faeries turned to him. "Song?" Nahtaia asked.

"You know, the children's song. 'Step into a faery ring, deaf to beats of faery wing. No way out and none to call, then charmed to dance until you fall.'"

Nahtaia and Oren looked at one another in surprise.

"Seems like the humans know more about us than they let on," Oren smirked.

"I'm curious how the rest of that song goes," she added.

They stepped out of the bush as the minotaurs disappeared into the trees.

"I'll tell you more someday," Kale said. "But until then, why don't we ask them for directions?"

"Are you mad?" Oren snapped. "Did you see the size of those things?"

"They're big, sure, but are they bad? I thought that minotaurs leaned more to the good side of Jaydür."

"Of course you'd think such a thing. You obviously don't know the world as well as you should. There are good minotaurs and bad minotaurs the same way there are good fae and bad fae. But *that* minotaur," he said, jabbing a finger at the bulls, "and the faery city, Lyra, do not stand on even ground since Nahtaia's handiwork. The ministers suffered a great amount of troubles this past week. They would be quicker to squish us than to help us."

"Tiny green man is right," a deep, rumbling voice spoke from behind. The trio looked up just in time to miss the first swing of the axe. Nahtaia screamed and took to the shrubs as Oren and Kale spread out in the other direction. The minotaur was after her.

"Much easier to catch when bug have no wings," he growled with a touch of pleasure in his tone, then swung his blade once more. Nahtaia dropped to her belly and felt the wind of the axe breathe on her back. She scrambled back up and kept running.

"Do you know how it feels to be under faery power?" he rumbled.

"It was your own fault!" she shouted over her shoulder, then slapped herself in the face for speaking. The minotaur roared and swung his weapon again, and Nahtaia saw she had no escape. She closed her eyes with a shriek as the blade cut the air. Instead of the sharp slice she expected, she was thrown to the ground, then felt the wind beneath her. She opened her eyes and looked up to see Oren.

"This is not the time to be opinionated, Bluebird," he said as he lifted her away from the creatures. An angry roar from the minotaur resonated through the woods, shaking the weaker leaves from their branches.

"What took you so long?" she cried.

He dropped her in a bird's nest just above the minotaurs' reach, then flew back down, muttering, "'What took you so long?' You're welcome." The second minotaur was shaking with laughter as he pointed at his friend, who'd missed his target.

Oren spotted Kale beside a boulder and as the first minotaur stomped toward the human, Oren readied his bow and arrow.

The poison would have no effect on such a large and powerful creature but it would distract the thing, so Oren took a shot. The minotaur kept walking until a second arrow stuck in his arm. He stopped, turned, and focused his big coal eyes on Oren. With a snotty grunt, he stamped the ground and charged toward him, axe readied. Oren raised an eyebrow and laughed at the thought that it actually expected to catch a faery. Then it happened. Five dirty, bulgy fingers snatched him from behind, just one squeeze away from being crushed. It was the second minotaur.

"Oren!" Nahtaia screamed. She instinctively searched for Kale and found him hidden, frozen in fear. He was just a human; he had no magic that could help.

The minotaur brought Oren to eye level and shook with laughter. "Little green man not so clever after all," he said. "Let this be reminder to other bug people never to make fools of my kind."

"I've said no—" Oren started before his air was squeezed out of him. His bones cracked, just shy of breaking.

Without thinking, Nahtaia leaped from the nest and landed on the minotaur's head but he didn't react. She held on to one of his horns and shouted to get the attention of the first one; the one who wanted to kill her more than anyone.

"Hey, you!" she shouted. "Charming you was easier than tipping a sleeping cow!"

Rage flickered in his eyes when he spotted her, and the second minotaur shook his head, trying to get her off. She held fast to his horn, digging her heels into his grizzly hide.

"I couldn't have done a better job if you were a swine!" she added with a giggle.

The first minotaur's roar was accompanied with a shower of saliva. He lurched forward trying to snatch her, but she dropped down the face of the second, gripping the metal ring that was pierced through his ear. A loud thump filled the air as the two made hard contact and the second minotaur fell to the ground. Nahtaia held on, then jumped off before the monstrous creature hit the earth. She saw Oren roll out of his hand, get up, and run to her. The first one spotted them and flung his axe when Oren gripped her around the waist and lifted her into the air.

"Stay here," he said breathlessly before flying back down. The minotaurs were arguing in their own tongue as he snuck up behind them. They didn't see him as he found Kale and flew him into the treetops as well. Nahtaia looked down from the branch she stood on and saw the creatures throw fists and tackle one another.

"Let's get out of here before they decide to take down the tree," she suggested.

"Agreed," Kale and Oren replied.

That evening, Nahtaia, Oren, and Kale came across a pond. At first, Oren wandered around trying to find shelter until he noticed something about the water. When Nahtaia dipped her hand in for a drink, it rippled from the outside, in rather than the inside out.

"We're all right for the night," he called with a grin. Nahtaia and Kale looked up from their conversation as he made his way to them. "It's an Aquinian well."

Nahtaia jumped up and hovered even closer over the water, searching. "Are you sure?"

"But the Aquinians are on the other side of Jaydür," Kale pointed out.

"So is the human territory," Oren grumbled.

Nahtaia narrowed her eyes at him in silent warning.

"These are nymphatic waters," Oren then added. "The Voice of Apan rested here at some point in her ageless existence. All creatures are protected from harm here."

Kale watched Nahtaia curiously as she lowered her head until her nose was less than an inch from the water. "Hello?" she said as she waved her hand. "I'd like to have a word with you, if you please."

Kale frowned. "You really think nymphs would show themselves?"

"Well, I can't very well leave here without at least trying. Nymphs can make direct contact with the Voice of Apan."

"That means," Oren cut in, "that this little journey of death would be done tonight if we were to speak with her."

"Exactly," Nahtaia said, then called again to the waters. "Please. I must speak with a Voice. You see, I think there's been a mistake."

Oren slapped a hand to his head with a groan. "You don't tell the Voices they've made a mistake, Nahtaia."

"That's not what I'm saying," she hissed in reply. "Stop talking. You're making me look bad."

"As you're speaking to your reflection in the water." Kale chuckled.

Nahtaia stuck out her tongue. After a few more minutes with no answer from the waters, she sat up with a sigh. "This is not fair."

"Just be glad we can make a fire tonight," Oren sighed as he rose to his feet. "I'm going to find some wood."

Kale lay down in the grass and after a few minutes of silence, he began to snore. Nahtaia pressed her lips into a tight line, finally knowing which one of the men had been making such a racket the last couple of nights. She rested on her belly with her head by the water and skimmed her fingers over the surface, watching the strange ripples. It *was* an Aquinian well, no doubt. Being one of the few in the world, she wondered how long ago it was created, as Aquinian wells showed no signs of age, much like everything else related to the Voices.

The wells were placed secretly among the different lands as subtle reminders of the existence of the Great

Four along with Folcavian torches, Windmills of Mae'Ehr, and D'Irdda Oaks. Each were places where the Voices had rested at some point in Jaydür's existence.

"He's out already," Oren said, laying down some twigs and leaves for the fire. "Humans."

"Must you be so rude to him all the time?" Nahtaia sighed, turning onto her back.

"He needs to learn his place, and by the way, I did save his life today, remember?"

Nahtaia bit her lip as she thought back, then remembered how close that minotaur's axe had come to cutting her in half. She looked to Oren as he worked and noticed something about his wing. She sat up with a frown and crawled beside him to look closer.

"They clipped your wing," she said.

Oren looked over his shoulder with a shrug. "Not enough to matter. I survived. And I can still fly."

"You jumped in front of that axe to save me."

Oren finally met her eyes with surprise on his face. "You noticed? It wasn't the first time I've saved your life, you know."

Nahtaia looked down at her hands, then to Kale before letting out a long sigh and whispering, "Thank you...again."

"And I'll do it again," he replied.

A blush rose to her face at his words and she looked away. "Quickly, let's change the subject before we bond or something."

Oren focused on increasing the fire, but there was a new air about him, a sense that he knew something she did not.

Chapter 10

Bluebird," Oren grinned, waiting for Nahtaia and Kale as they climbed through a row of thorn bushes. "Do you love me?"

Nahtaia took a deep, exasperated breath as she carefully ducked and stepped along the way. He'd been asking that question since the other day with the minotaur run-in. "Oren, give it up."

"The guy just wants a straight answer," Kale interjected. "It's not so easy for us men to figure these things out."

"Oren knows very well there is nothing to figure out," she replied, just as she was about to get out of the shrubs herself. She was jerked sideways and Kale pointed to the ground at a shard of glass she hadn't seen. "Thank you," she said as they both stepped out of the bush. "Phew!" she huffed. "I say we try letting Kale lead."

Oren wrinkled his nose as if smelling something sour. "Why?" he asked, readjusting his bow and quiver on his bare back.

"Because just today you led us through a gorge, an old dwarven camp and a thorn trap. That's why."

"I agree," Kale added, picking some leaves out of Nahtaia's hair.

"Thank you," she replied, then followed after him.

"You know, you've thanked Kale at least five times more than you've thanked me our entire lives together," Oren pointed out.

"I don't know what you're talking about," Nahtaia said.

Traveling so long with nothing but the same type of scenery—birch trees and the promise of more birch trees—was taking a toll on the trio. Nahtaia's feet calloused so much that she felt nothing as she walked on dirt and rocks, though she still felt the thorns. The road ahead looked the same, but the men were acting differently and Nahtaia began to wonder…and worry.

Oren was strangely quiet as he walked behind the pair. He insisted on remaining behind them, saying, "With a human in the lead, a death trap is sure to follow." In Oren-speak, that was his way of saying he was going to protect them.

Oaf, Nahtaia thought. And at that thought, she really began to worry because something happened: she felt guilt. He had saved her life numerous times, after all.

What does it matter? she thought. *He's doing it for his own gain, just like always. He wants to be looked upon as a shiny hero when we get back.* And yet, just the thought made that guilt rise all the more like bile in her throat, as if he deserved recognition and she was realizing it again. She huffed in annoyance with herself.

Apparently, the guilt wasn't the worst part. The hairs on the back of her neck stood on end, and when she looked over her shoulder—Oren was staring at her. She turned back but the prickles would not cease. She looked over again with a frown, and he was still staring, but this time one side of his lips pulled up into a half-smile. Nahtaia clenched her fists and realized Kale also watched her with a quizzical brow. She wrinkled her forehead and looked forward, flexing her jaw.

More prickles...and silence.

She couldn't take it any longer. Nahtaia stopped, stamped her feet, and hissed, "Stop staring at me!" then walked faster. The men exchanged confused glances.

"Is she going to be all right?" Kale asked, looking after her.

"Let's hope so," Oren replied.

The next day, the forest finally cleared. Through one last row of pines, a vast and empty sea of grass spread before them. There was nothing on the horizon and Nahtaia felt sick to her stomach. Were they even going the right way? All she knew was the Elven Territory was to the west. She had hoped to see, at the very least, the leaves of the Willow of D'Irdda. If a tree as massive as an Elven willow could not be seen, they were still a very, very long way away.

"You don't suppose there is a non-faery-eating bird we can ride on, do you?" Nahtaia huffed.

"No," Oren laughed. "I don't."

She sighed and made her way to a tree, skimming her eyes over the trunk from the bottom up.

"What are you looking for?" Kale asked, then took a bite out of a berry he'd picked.

"A way up," she replied.

Kale looked to Oren, then back at her. "And why do you want to go up the tree?"

"To find out if there is anything besides a field in the distance."

Oren flew up into the treetops.

"Or he can find out," she sighed and dropped to the ground. Pressing her palms on her eyes, she began to think, to remember. "Kale, remember when you were showing me your statue?"

Kale sat beside her, cross-legged, and nodded.

"It seems like forever has passed," she added. "As if it never happened. But I liked those days. I really did." She leaned back onto her hands and blankly looked up. "Life was so simple. The worst I ever had to think about was the next time Oren would be within my line of sight. Now it's all about survival and getting my magic and wings back and having Oren there constantly."

"You know," Kale interrupted, "it seems like your life revolves around him and always has."

"Who?"

"Oren."

Nahtaia bristled at the thought. "Here I am trying to have a nice, intelligent conversation with you and you make it about Oren."

"I'm not making it about him, you are. You always have."

Nahtaia got up with a groan and stomped off into the field. How dare he talk to her like that? What happened to the days when they were friends? The days when they could talk about life and his work and family. She remembered how easy it was to get along with him and how careful he was not to hurt her feelings or make her feel uncomfortable. Now they were out in the wild and he was either not speaking at all or making her feel foolish. Where had things changed?

"Probably when you surprised him with being a faery," she muttered in response to her own thoughts. "Stupid Willy."

She planted her feet and crossed her arms, staring off into the grass. The sky was clouded in gray, warning of more wet weather to come. A dark sky was never good for the fae. Any predatory birds could be soaring about, looking for their next meal and would easily go unnoticed. Three tiny people would be an easy pick from the field.

"Excuse me," a small muffled voice spoke, bringing her to the surface from deep thought. Nahtaia froze and skimmed the area but saw no one.

"Yes?" she replied.

"I'm sorry, but you're on my exit," the voice said. Nahtaia frowned and jumped when the ground beneath her shook. She stepped back with a hand on her heart and watched as a small metal tool broke through the ground. The earth crumbled around the tool as it pushed side to side, making an opening just big enough for a small man-like creature to lift himself out. It was an earthmover.

"Thank you," the earthmover said with a slight bow of his head. He clapped dirt off his hands and took up his tool again, hitching it onto his shoulder, then looked up to her with a smile. "Greetings," he said.

"Greetings," she replied, studying the man. His clothes were caked in dirt; understandable, since earthmovers did live underground. He was about an inch shorter than she was—which put him at three inches tall—but he was well built. Wiry hairs covered his arms, the skin taut over brawny muscle. His brown hair was tied back at his short neck, also covered in dirt and dust.

"I'm Dweegen," he said with a bow. "Earthmover."

"I'm Nahtaia," she replied. "Faery."

He furrowed his brow as his eyes searched the empty air above her shoulders. "A faery without wings?" He chuckled. "That's like an earthmover without a pick."

"Ironic, isn't it?" she replied, her mind suddenly distracted with the possibility that this man knew where they were. "Excuse me, but can you tell me where we are?"

"Nahtaia!" Kale called, a twinge of panic in his voice. Oren dropped down beside her, flustered and out of breath while Kale ran up from behind. A tight-lipped grin appeared on Dweegen's face, scrunching his eyes, as everyone came together.

"'Ello and greetings," he said with another bow. The men replied with winded hellos and turned back to Nahtaia. "By the Highest Power," Oren huffed. "Do you have any idea the panic I just went through?"

Nahtaia chewed on her lip and threw Oren a distracted glance. "We'll discuss it later; right now, I'm trying to find out where we are."

Kale studied the man from head to toe before he looked back to Nahtaia. "I'm sorry," he whispered as Oren spoke with the earthmover. "I didn't mean to offend you when we spoke about Oren. I suppose I'm just tired from this whole journey. I was rude."

Nahtaia looked him in the eyes and could see the sincerity from days passed; the sincerity that she missed from the carving-lesson days. "It's all right," she replied with a small smile, then turned to listen to Dweegen.

"...strange we should run into one another," he was saying to Oren. "I've been traveling with my family and decided to get ahead while they rested. We're going to see some of our extended family about a mile east of here."

"Do you have any notion of how far we stand from the Willow of D'Irdda?" Oren asked, arms crossed.

Dweegen's eyes widened and he let out a bellow of laughter. "The Willow of D'Irdda? Why, that's ages from here. That's on the other side of Jaydür!"

Upon hearing Dweegen's response, Nahtaia's teeth and fists instantly clenched. "But we *can* get there sooner. There *is* a way." Kale placed a hand on her shoulder and she stepped forward. "No," she snapped. "There is a way, and I'm going to find it."

Dweegen looked down at her with a serious frown, looking worried about what he'd said to upset her. "Is something wrong?"

Oren interlaced his fingers behind his head and took a long, deep breath before saying, "A bit. We're trying to reach the elves so we can get Nahtaia's wings back."

When Kale started to speak, Oren quickly cut him off with a casual wave of his hand and said, "Oh, and turn the human back to his natural size."

Dweegen nodded in understanding, then rubbed his scruffy chin in thought. "Do any of you three have an aversion to small dark spaces?" Dweegen asked.

Nahtaia was deep in thought, her gaze settled on a blade of grass swaying in the breeze, while the men answered, "No."

"Oh, good," Dweegen continued. "We have a tunnel in the direction of Gaia Faults, just short of the Great Willow. I can get you a ride there, if you'd be willing to do something for me, that is."

There was an odd, unnatural tone to his voice that caught Nahtaia's attention. She looked up to find the earthmover smiling a crooked, dirty smile at something in her direction. Wait, was he looking at her?

"What do you need?" Oren asked, following his gaze, which settled on Nahtaia with raised brows.

Dweegen wrung his short, chubby, hairy hands. With a clearing of his throat, a blush claimed his cheeks as he said, "A kiss, from the fair faery."

"What?" she snapped.

"Oh boy," Oren sighed, putting a hand to his head.

A wave of anger swept through Nahtaia. Her blood ran hot and her hands tingled. Kale looked down at her, surprised at such a request from a stranger, but Oren knew better. Nahtaia needed to be held back.

In the blink of an eye, she was in mid-air, jumping toward the earthmover, armed with teeth and fingernails. He let out a feminine shriek and recoiled just before Oren snatched her from the air and held her fast.

"How dare you!" Nahtaia snapped. "After all that I have been through!"

"Why a kiss?" Kale asked.

Dweegen swallowed hard and nervously glanced between Nahtaia and Kale. "Everyone knows a faery kiss will bring you good fortune."

Oren laughed and replied, "I think it'd have to be a kiss from a good-tempered faery. A kiss from Nahtaia may be the death of you."

"Well, I can't help you if I don't get what I want in return!" Dweegen exclaimed, turning back to his hole.

"No, no, no!" Oren yelled, then looked to Nahtaia. "Bluebird," he said in his sing-song tone that he used when he would tease her. "We can really use a ride."

Nahtaia fought against him, trying to pull away, but he was too strong. "I will not kiss anyone, thank you very much," she objected. "Where do either of you get the nerve to ask such a thing?"

Kale turned to Oren and frowned. "Isn't there another way?"

"I know what I want, and that's some good fortune," Dweegen said.

"But look at her. She really doesn't want to. It's not fair to ask something like that of her."

"It's just a kiss," Oren snapped. "One small kiss and—" he paused and turned to Dweegen. "Where do you want it?"

Nahtaia's face twisted in disgust when the earthmover licked his lips and pointed to the corner of them. "Right here."

"I am *not*—" she started as Oren moved her toward Dweegen.

"Nahtaia, please," Oren groaned. "Would you rather walk all the way? We can catch up on our rest and get to the elves faster. The sooner we get there, the sooner you get your wings and magic back, the sooner Kale is gone and the sooner you and I get to go home and sleep in our beds. Which part about that *doesn't* sound pleasant?"

Oren released his hold on her and after a moment, she stepped toward the earthmover. With the tension and unwillingness of the situation, she noticed everything unpleasant about the man. His bushy eyebrows that seemed like they crossed from eye to eye without a break; the small dark hairs that covered the majority of his face; the dirt caking the corners of his lips, which happened to be the one place he wanted her to kiss. She was, all in all, disgusted with the very notion, but she did want to get the journey over and done with.

Dweegen waited expectantly, his chest puffed with pride.

With a deep intake of breath, Nahtaia leaned down and gave the man a peck on the corner of his lips. Without another thought, she spun on her heel and hooked onto Kale's arm. Being the only one who thought about her feelings on the situation, he'd earned himself some new respect. He looked down at her with a soft smile and even a light blush.

"Can we go now?" she curtly asked the earthmover.

Dweegen rose his head high with a grin as he motioned down toward his hole. "After you," he said.

Chapter 11

Underground was no place for faeries. The air was stuffy and thick with an uncomfortable heat that wrapped around them like a cocoon. Though Dweegen could stand up straight in the tunnel, Oren, Kale, and Nahtaia walked with a slight slouch. Kale was directly behind the earthmover while Oren insisted on taking up the rear again. Nahtaia was caught in the middle as usual.

The one positive thing about being underground was the lack of thorns and rocks. Just smooth, cool dirt made up the ceiling, walls, and ground they walked on.

"So the lovely lady did have wings?" Dweegen asked.

"At one point," Oren replied from the back. Nahtaia tried to ignore the sound of his voice, as she was still rather touchy about the kiss ordeal. Kale was silent most of the way, throwing an occasional glance over his shoulder at Nahtaia. She smiled once at him and he seemed to fight a grin.

"May I ask what happened, that a bare back came to be?" the earthmover went on.

Oren was about to respond before Nahtaia cut in. "A snake tore them off just after I'd kissed a twit."

She let out a squeak of disapproval when Oren pegged her with a wad of dirt.

"What?" she hissed over her shoulder. When she turned back, she nearly bumped into Kale. Dweegen had stopped moving and stood staring wide-eyed at the faeries.

"That's not good fortune at all," he mumbled and continued on his way.

The rest of the walk was quiet. Dweegen continued to ramble incoherently under his breath and the three followed on. Nearly an hour passed with no sign of change in the tunnel.

Small torches lit the way, making Nahtaia wonder who else was around, but she didn't bother asking. Dweegen seemed to take every excuse to chatter incessantly when given the chance.

Nahtaia's back started to hurt from all the hunching over. Just as she was about to voice her complaints, Dweegen stopped and the three travelers stopped behind him.

"What is—" she started before Dweegen shushed her. She wrinkled her nose in offense, then frowned, following everyone's gaze. The wall shuddered, causing the roof to crumble, little by little. A sound like a rake on dirt came from the rear of the group, where Oren stood. He stepped forward and touched the wall curiously, then jumped back when it shook once, harder.

Dweegen's running footsteps drew their attention, and Kale, Oren, and Nahtaia all exchanged looks of confusion. Not a foot below the ceiling, a small ball of dirt fell from the wall to the ground, and a hole opened just enough for something long and pink to poke through. The end of the thing was split in two and kept moving in and out of the hole.

Another shudder.

"By the Highest Power," Oren whispered. He pushed Nahtaia forward, bumping her into Kale, forcing them to move. "Go," he said. "Go!"

The tunnel shook again as they began running, and a pointed snake nose broke through the ground. Its beady eyes locked on the group as it quickly slithered forward. The three ran faster, soon spotting Dweegen in the distance. He peeked over his shoulder and held onto his hat as he pushed his legs harder. Oren struggled to ready his bow in the tight tunnel. Nahtaia looked back, glimpsing the two nostrils and protruding fangs of the burrowing snake gaining ground quickly.

"You had to say something about a snake," Oren huffed from behind.

"I wasn't serious!" Nahtaia replied.

The snake raised its head to the ceiling, then pounded it on the tunnel floor, sending violent tremors through the earth. Dweegen kept his balance for the most part, but the rest were having a difficult time staying on their feet.

"This is not good fortune at all," Dweegen cried.

"Just keep going!" prodded Kale. "Oren, can't you shoot it?"

"No!" Dweegen shrieked. "It's bad fortune to kill a—"

"Oh, shut it with your fortune!" Nahtaia snapped. "Oren, shoot it!"

Oren got the arrow on the bow but lost his grip when the snake pounded the ground again.

"Now you've got butterfingers?" she growled. "It's coming!"

"We're running out of escape routes," Dweegen cried as he came to a full stop. "I can't lead it to my family. I have children!"

Oren managed to shoot off an arrow but missed the eye just as the snake raised its head. He turned to Nahtaia with hard eyes, his face wrinkled in desperation. There wasn't enough time to ready another arrow on the bow. She frowned as he turned away, then ran toward the snake. It took her a second to realize what he was doing.

"Oren!" she shrieked and tried to run after him, but Kale snatched her by the wrist.

"He'll be fine!" he assured her.

Oren leaped toward the snake, arrow in hand, landing on the ground just beneath it. The head slammed down hard and fast, then after a fit of shaking, lay unmoving with the arrow in its throat.

Nahtaia, Kale, and Dweegen stared at the creature, waiting for Oren to move. Nothing happened.

"Please be okay," Nahtaia whispered. She pulled away from Kale and ran toward the animal. Thinking about what just happened, she knew the head was big and came down heavily enough to smash any faery.

"Oren?" she cried, shoving the snake's head as hard as she could. All the memories of her life and the jokes she played on him crowded her mind. "Kale, help me! Oren?"

Kale joined her, followed by Dweegen, and with all three trying, they lifted the snake's head and dropped it beside an unconscious Oren. Nahtaia kneeled down beside him and brushed away the dirt on his face. His skin was cold and blood came from a cut on his brow. She looked up at Kale and Dweegen with tears in her eyes and shook her head.

"Oren," she said, shaking him. "Please."

He didn't move.

"Does he have a pulse?" Kale asked.

She looked up at him with a frown. "A what?"

"A pulse. Is he breathing?"

Nahtaia swallowed hard and put her hand just below his nose. Her shoulders dropped with her last bit of hope when she felt no breath. She stared at Oren as images of a future without his hassling and annoying presence played in her mind. She didn't want it to end like this. If only she'd been kinder. She'd imagined a world without Oren several times in her life, but if she had known it would actually happen, maybe she would have found a way to not be annoyed by him. Maybe she even would have tried to be friends. But it was too late for that now.

Goosebumps rose all over her body. Her mind was not working. She couldn't think or move or talk. She could only stare at the body of the man who spent the vast majority of his years following and hounding her. The man she'd rejected in every way imaginable.

"Nahtaia," Kale tried, but she recoiled from his touch.

"We really should go," Dweegen whispered as he surveyed the snake corpse. "Other predators may smell the blood."

"We can't just leave him here," Nahtaia snapped, looking up at Kale. He was staring at Oren with narrowed eyes. She frowned, and the moment she looked back at Oren, her lips met with his. For about three seconds she didn't realize what was happening but then scrambled back onto her feet, pushing Oren back down. He didn't seem to mind, as he was suffering a fit of laughter.

"You—" she started, out of breath. "You're not—but—"

Oren finally got up, his face wet with tears from laughing so hard. She stared at him and felt the blood rise in her face.

"Oh, Nahtaia," he said, still grinning. "You should have seen your face."

"But you weren't breathing," she said so quietly she wondered if anyone heard her.

He wiped his face with his hands when Nahtaia was suddenly on him like a rabid dog on a hare, knocking him right back down to the ground. She grabbed his neck and shook him, pounding the back of his head into the earth.

"You rotten toadstool!" she shrieked. "I'm going to kill you!"

He rolled her over, holding her by her wrists and grinning. "I finally got what I've been wanting. I can die a happy man now."

She nearly blushed but gave a swift and strong knee to his groin instead. He was quickly disarmed then and easy to push away.

"That was the most horrid idea of a joke, Oren!" she cried. "I will never forgive you for this. You have lost any and all respect I have ever felt toward you."

"Looks like we're back on track," Kale replied.

"You are a rather odd group," Dweegen added with a sigh.

Hours later, the group reached the end of the tunnel. They made one stop on the way at Dweegen's home, where he quickly introduced his family, then led them on in the right direction. His wife was a bit nervous when she saw the blood on Oren's head, but her husband assured her everyone was well.

Nahtaia refused to look Oren in the eyes. How could he have done something so cold and heartless to her? Just when positive thoughts about him were finding their way into her mind after hating him for so long, too. Now he was as far away as any unimportant thought. Or so she told herself. Until that death stunt of his, she thought she hated him with every fiber of her being. Now she was utterly confused. New feelings at the thought of his death arose, but they didn't make any sense. Maybe it was just because of the journey to the elves. Maybe she was just reacting to the sense of him being gone during the trip. He was their only weapon, after all.

The air outside the tunnel was comforting after so many hours underground. The sun was melting into the horizon where, to Nahtaia's pleasure, the tips of enormous leaves and branches of a great willow peeked through gray clouds. Dweegen insisted upon them staying with him for the night, but Oren assured him he'd find a safe shelter *above* ground.

"Well," Dweegen sighed, patting the dirt off his hands. "I guess I'll see you in the morning. I'll be here early to get your transportation set up."

"Thank you," the three replied.

The earthmover bowed his head and disappeared back into his hole. Nahtaia's eyes were locked on the willow as a new hope rose within her. If she could see any part of the willow, that meant they made some distance. It wouldn't be too long before they met the elves.

"I'll be back, Bluebird," Oren said as he jumped into the air and went off to explore the area for shelter.

"Are you all right?" Kale asked.

She turned to him with a small smile. "I'm fine."

He shifted his weight onto his other leg and cleared his throat. "Well, you know. Because of what happened."

Nahtaia raised a brow and couldn't help thinking how adorable Kale was sometimes. He was so concerned about hurting her feelings or bringing up uncomfortable topics.

"What, the kiss?" She smirked, trying to seem nonchalant about the memory. "Pfft, like he's—"

"Not the kiss," Kale cut in. "What he did was wrong. It was horrible. I don't believe that you're okay with it."

She turned away and shrugged. "It's not the first time he's done something stupid."

"That was more than just stupid but—" he paused, and Nahtaia could sense he wanted to say more.

"But what?" She sighed, turning to him. She waited for him to continue.

"I found a place," Oren said, dropping down beside them. His chest was still puffed along with his ego. "Ready?"

"Where is it this time?" Kale asked.

"In a tree, as usual," he replied. Kale's eyes darted between Oren and Nahtaia as Oren's gaze was fixated on her. He looked back at Kale and winked before grabbing her and lifting her over his shoulder. "I'll take you first."

"Oren!" she protested for a moment, but then hung loosely over his shoulder, as she knew nothing she could say would stop him.

The two were airborne for a moment before Oren put her back on her feet in front of an old squirrel den. She pulled away from him and started toward the entrance, but he flew over her and blocked the way. "So?" he said, bracing himself against the sides of the hole. Nahtaia frowned and put her hands on her hips.

"So what?" she asked.

"So what did you think?"

"About which part?" she snapped. "You giving me a heart attack or your kiss of death?"

He considered her response. "Both."

"I think you're a selfish troll who cares about no one but yourself."

He raised a hand to move some hair out of her eyes, but she slapped him away. "Okay, I changed my mind," he continued. "Let's focus on the kiss. Did you like it?"

"No. Don't flatter yourself. I'd hardly call *that* a kiss, anyway."

He smiled so widely that dimples formed on both cheeks. He lowered his eyes for a moment before he stepped forward, biting his lower lip. "Can I try again?" He looked up through his lashes, locking his gaze on hers.

Blood rushed to Nahtaia's face and she swallowed hard. Was the fool being serious?

In the silence, an owl screeched and Nahtaia's focus faltered. As soon as it did, Oren stepped forward, cupping her face in his hands and bringing his lips to hers. Nahtaia froze the moment his breath caressed her face. The strong woodsy scent she remembered from back when he'd first carried her to a shelter in the trees entered her nostrils and her senses came alive. As their lips molded and moved together, it felt as if every pore in her body, from scalp to toes, opened at once and a wave of cool air washed over her. Heat burst in her blood, starting from where his warm hands held her face, contrasting strangely to the coldness of her skin. Her heart palpitated.

"Hello?" Kale's voice reached them from below, snapping Nahtaia back to reality. She shoved against Oren and stepped away, taken aback by her own response to his kiss.

"You charmed me," she said, wrapping her arms around her herself. She was shuddering. Was it cold? "You're not supposed to charm your own kind." Her eyes stung with brimming tears.

"I didn't charm you," he said. He looked serious, but a smile still hinted at his mouth. She didn't believe him.

"How could you?" she whispered. She pushed past him and pointed down. "Go get Kale. If you say a word, I'll—" She choked on her words as she hurried into the den.

Oren followed her inside. "I didn't charm you," he repeated. "I would never do that."

"Oh please, Oren," she growled. "I'm not as stupid as you think I am! Go get Kale and leave me be."

"I don't think—"

"Where did this come from?" she cried. "We fight all the time. When did we start kissing?" She covered her face with her hands. "This is absurd."

Oren gently pulled her hands from her face. She jerked away at his touch and pushed his hands away.

"Stop touching me," she demanded.

"Listen to me," he begged. "I don't think you're stupid. I never did. How could you accuse me of charming you?"

"Because that didn't feel normal. That was confusing and strange. What *was* that?" she asked, flailing her hands in the air.

"Uh, I don't know, maybe you *liked* it." He spoke the words as if the whole world knew something she didn't. She stared at him and shook her head, not knowing how to respond. She couldn't have simply liked it. The feelings she suffered were not comfortable. He had to have charmed her. She wouldn't accept any other answer.

With a deep breath and hardened eyes, she turned away and said, "Go get Kale, Oren."

Chapter 12

The night would not pass quickly, and to make it worse, there was no moon. The den was pitch black and Nahtaia jumped at every movement from the men. After Oren had brought Kale from the ground, she insisted they both sleep on the opposite side of the den. She would not have another man touch her. Oren scoffed at the thought but did as was requested. Kale gave her a bit more of a hard time, not because he wanted to sleep beside her but because he was concerned.

Eyes wide and ears attentive, Nahtaia stared into the darkness. Even though she knew where the men were sleeping, she couldn't see them and that made her uncomfortable. Her mind was spinning with what happened just before they settled for the night.

Refusing to believe she actually enjoyed such a repugnant and bold move from Oren, she continued to accuse him of charming her. There was no way it could have been anything less than that. Magic was definitely at work.

"Nahtaia?" A voice broke through the darkness, followed by a frustrated sigh. "Are you all right?" It was Oren. Why wasn't he sleeping?

She didn't respond at first, hoping he'd think she was asleep and would drop whatever it was he wanted to say.

Something shifted in the shadows, and he whispered her name again.

"No," she hissed in reply. "Leave me alone. Go to sleep."

At the first sound of her voice, she could hear him making his way to her.

"Stay there," she demanded, recoiling into the bark behind her.

He flitted his wings just enough to make his flight-light fade off and on to help him through the dark. With her heart in her throat, she quickly covered her eyes with her hands. Heat came from his body along with the woodsy smell of his breath as he settled on the floor beside her.

"What are you doing?" he asked.

"I told you to stay there," she said.

"Why are you covering your eyes?"

"I don't make the same mistake twice, birdbrain. You can't charm me if we don't meet eyes."

He let out a breath, grabbed her wrists and jerked her hands off her face. "I didn't charm you," he said. "You know me better than that."

With her eyes still squeezed shut, she wrinkled her nose in annoyance. "I know you enough not to trust you."

"If you didn't trust me, you wouldn't let me be around this long."

She swallowed hard and finally opened her eyes. With the fluttering of his wings, his light was just enough to envelop both of them. He touched her chin and lifted her face to look at him, but her eyes remained downcast.

"Nahtaia, I'm not going to do anything," he said. When she still refused, he let out a growl. "Is it so hard for you to accept that you might just have some feelings for me?"

At that, she snapped her eyes to his. "I do not!" she objected. "That's preposterous."

"You do; you just don't know how to handle it. You've always been bad with your emotions. They go up and down with the waxing and waning of the moon. I know you more than anyone in Lyra. That's where your discomfort came from—not knowing what you were feeling."

"You don't know anything about me, Oren."

"You didn't react when the human over there kissed you," Oren finally pointed out.

She rolled onto her other side, curling up into a ball. "You wouldn't know whether or not I reacted."

He leaned down and whispered in her ear, "I was watching you. You walked away."

Again she remained quiet, remembering the day when Kale showed interest in her. More recently, he'd almost been ignoring her. Maybe he finally gave up. Though that thought was a bit sad, it would be for the best, if it was true.

When Oren saw she wasn't responding, he lay down on his back. "You kissed *me* back."

Nahtaia shot up onto her bottom and glared down at him. "I did not."

"You did too. I remember." He licked his lips and added, "I was there."

"Arguing with you is pointless," she said as she rose to her feet and felt her way around him.

Sitting up, Oren fluttered his wings again, lighting the area just briefly enough for Nahtaia to find her way to the other side of the den where Kale slept. Nahtaia wondered how in the world humans could sleep through so much talk and movement. She'd have beaten her neighbors with a stick if they talked so much while she was trying to sleep.

"We'll help you work through your feelings, Bluebird," Oren said as he finally settled in for the night. "I have no doubts."

The morning came with rain—so much of it that the ground flooded to the point that Oren was not willing to take the chance of traveling on foot. Nahtaia kneeled on the branch, looking below. Her hope fell more with every drop of rain that pitter-pattered onto the ground.

"I can't believe this," she whimpered. She was looking forward to walking off some frustration. The last thing she wanted was to be stuck in a tiny den with Oren.

"Nahtaia," Kale called from the entrance to the den. "Shouldn't you come inside? I mean—"

"We have to be able to go," she said. "Where's the earthmover?"

Kale turned to Oren, who sat on the ground with his back against the wall of the tree. A grin stretched from ear to ear and Kale sighed.

"Oren spoke with him this morning," Kale said.

Nahtaia quickly got to her feet and stomped into the den. "You did what?" she barked.

"He'll be here as soon as the rain stops," Oren explained with his hands behind his head. He was so smug, it made her sick. She paced the length of the den with her fists clenched and nostrils flared.

"Oren," she started. "We have to get to the elves. We have to fix things. I can't be wingless and magicless forever."

"We'll get there," Kale said gently, trying to comfort her.

Oren chuckled. "Are you blaming the rain on me?"

"We could have traveled farther underground," she replied through clenched teeth. "We could have worked something out." She stopped at the doorway and rubbed her jaw. Over the last few days, there was a lot of jaw-clenching and now her face was sore.

"Can't you go find Dweegen?" Kale asked Oren. "It's not like it's too late to go down there."

"The earthmover is with his family," Oren explained. "It would be rude for us to interfere."

Kale glanced between Nahtaia and Oren. His face suddenly became flustered and his chest rose and fell heavily with every breath before he burst out, "You just have to make things hard," he snapped. "Everything has to go your way, doesn't it?"

Nahtaia frowned and looked over her shoulder. Kale had two clenched fists at his sides, and Oren looked up at him from the ground.

"Excuse me?" Oren replied, his voice thick and deep.

"You're such a fool," Kale scoffed. "If you cared half as much as you claim, you'd see how much you're hurting her. No matter what she says, you do the opposite. When she wants something, you have to twist it into something else for yourself."

Oren stood up with an angry glint in his olive eyes. "Watch yourself, human."

"Kale," Nahtaia said as she stepped forward. She was surprised he had even spoken in the first place. "Let me deal—"

"Nahtaia knows me well enough," Oren interrupted. "She knows who I am and how I—"

"But all these years she didn't know you have feelings for her, did she?" He shook his head and let out a disappointed *humph*. "She knew my feelings within days. You're pathetic."

"Says the worthless human who left her trapped in a jar. Please. You have nothing to fight me with."

The muscles in Kale's arm twitched. Just as Nahtaia was about to interrupt their arguing, she screamed instead when Kale flung his fist into Oren's face. Oren stumbled back in shock before leaping back at Kale. Suddenly the two were rolling around on the ground in a ball of fists.

"Stop it!" Nahtaia cried. "You're both fools! Stop it this instant!"

She was ignored as they continued with their fight. Oren had Kale by the throat before Kale kneed him in the gut. They both landed a few punches, one making Oren's nose bleed and another cutting Kale's right eyebrow.

"Oren! Kale!" Nahtaia shouted, trying to pry them apart. "Both of you idiots! Can't you grow up?" She grabbed Oren's arm and pulled with all her strength, but he hardly moved from Kale. She was getting nowhere.

"You know what?" she cried, not caring anymore about holding back her tears. She'd been strong long enough and stresses were piling up. "I don't need either of you." She turned and stepped out onto the branch.

"Nahtaia," both men called just as she was climbing down the tree trunk.

There was another quick scuffle, complete with "shut your mouth" and "leave her alone." Nahtaia shook her head and continued her way down. Kale kneeled and called for her as Oren fluttered down beside her.

"What are you doing?" he asked in a rather demanding tone.

"What am *I* doing? What are *you* doing?" she sniffed, trying to cover her tone with a false laugh. "Go home, Oren." She wouldn't look up at him like this. She couldn't remember if he'd ever actually seen her cry. "I don't need you."

His laugh echoed in the forest. "We've had *this* talk."

"Kale's right," she said, planting her feet on whatever holes and extending bark she could set them on. "You're pathetic. Not that *he's* any better. You're both fools, getting in a fight like that."

"Nahtaia," Kale called from above. "Come back! I'm sorry!"

Oren glared at him, made an inappropriate faery gesture, and turned back to Nahtaia.

"I mean, you shouldn't even be here," she went on. "You have nothing to gain. You didn't shrink Kale, I did." She glanced over her shoulder at Oren and quickly regretted it. Her eyes were red and her face was flushed. There's no way he would miss the emotion lying behind it. "With your reputation, you could go to the ministers and tell them you've just been looking for me but didn't find me. They'd believe you and you could go on with your life."

"Nahtaia," he started.

She searched for a lower foothold and missed it, nearly losing her grip of the bark and scratching her cheek. She let out a cry and looked down at the great distance between herself and the ground. A subtle gasp escaped her lips when Oren's arms wrapped around her waist, supporting some of her weight.

"I'm sorry," he said. His breath was hot on her ear, raising goosebumps all over her body in the chill weather. "For all of this."

She couldn't come up with any witty remark. There was a sudden newfound trust in his apology, as if she could tell he actually meant it. But the moment was awkward and something had to be said.

"I'm going underground," she stated.

Oren sighed. "Not a good idea," he said with a shake of his head. "I didn't speak to the earthmover for my own reasons or pleasure. Kale doesn't even know what was said." He paused to look up at Kale, who'd begun his own descent. "The tunnel is in danger of collapsing in this weather," he went on. "I spoke to Dweegen moments before the rain actually started. Now the hole is full of water."

Nahtaia looked down but was too far up to see the hole. "So what are we supposed to do?" she asked with a twinge of panic in her voice.

"We wait out the storm."

She shook her head briskly and tried to climb down faster. "No. You and Kale are just going to fight or it's going to be awkward silence all the time. Whatever will be, it's going to be uncomfortable."

Bark rained down on the two and they looked up to see Kale holding on for his life.

Oren rolled his eyes.

"Go help him," Nahtaia said with a sigh. "I'm fine."

"No. Why should I?"

"Oren!" Nahtaia said, resting her forehead against the trunk.

"You know," Oren scoffed, "I'm thinking of just leaving him out here by himself. Ever since you've been wingless, we've become closer."

"We're not closer. Nothing has changed."

"When *he* showed up," he jabbed his finger toward Kale and spoke through clenched teeth, "things changed. Some for the better and some for the worse. I'm taking this opportunity to make *everything* better for you and me and our future."

"We don't have a future, Oren. Not what you're hoping for, at least."

"I'm not so sure about that," he said before flying off to help Kale.

Chapter 13

Awkward.

Nahtaia stared at the ground with her arms and legs crossed, shivering, her hair damp from the rain. Oren was at her right sitting against the wall, glaring at Kale with what could only be described as a deathly stare. Kale's eyes were settled on Nahtaia, concern etched on his face.

The rain fell harder and stronger a moment before she had begun her ascent back to the den after Oren saved Kale from falling. She had refused Oren's help and by the time she got inside, she was drenched head to toe, with every muscle in her body aching. Her hair stuck to her face and shoulders in waves like the bluest ocean.

"I thought faeries were cold-blooded," Kale said, breaking the silence when he noticed her shivering.

Everything about Oren constricted, ready to jump at the next sign of idiocy from the human. "Magic helps our bodies retain the needed temperature," he snapped, then turned sad eyes to Nahtaia. "No magic, no warmth in the cold and no cool in the heat."

"Nahtaia," Kale said, "maybe you should—"

"I'm fine," she replied quietly before he could finish.

"It's okay to accept help to make things more comfortable," Kale quietly added with a sad undertone.

Nahtaia said nothing. She knew what he meant, but she also knew she was a different faery now. When once she felt so full of life and fire, she now sat quiet and withdrawn. She was *tired,* and life's fervor washed away, along with the light of the moon in her skin.

"My troubles have not lessened since we left, and instead of you two getting along, you fight because of *me*. I don't know how to make it stop."

Kale and Oren both started to speak, interrupting one another; then Oren shook his head, stood, and made his way to the den entrance. Nahtaia looked up, weary and still upset with the whole feud.

Oren said nothing before he flew off through the rain. Kale sighed and stretched his legs out in front of him, looking up at Nahtaia through his lashes. "Look—"

"You hit him," she said with a small voice. Her eyes remained on a knot in the wood floor of the den and she smirked. "I didn't think you were brave enough to fight."

He ran a hand through his hair. "Only if it's worth it," he replied.

"It's easy to fight with Oren," she acknowledged. "He seems to bring out that side of people." When she looked up at him, she wrinkled her brow. Kale's face was pallid and a lustrous glaze spread across his eyes. Sweat beaded his hairline and she wondered how anyone could be sweating in such chilly weather. Kale watched her curiously as she crawled to him with a frown.

"What is it?" he asked.

"Are you okay?" she said, taking his face and tilting it to look at him in better light. When she felt his skin, she quickly pulled back. "You're so hot!"

He put a hand to his head. "It's just a fever. I felt it coming last night."

A panic overcame Nahtaia so suddenly that she didn't know how to react. "You mean, you're ill?" Her voice cracked at the last word.

He nodded, then shrugged. "I'll be fine."

"No, no. I've heard things about 'fevers,'" she whined. "They can be dangerous."

Kale laughed and raised his eyebrows. "Dangerous?"

She put a hand to his head, and Kale watched as her face changed from concerned to horrified. He took her hand from his head and said, "Nahtaia, it's nothing. It'll go away on its own. It always does."

Images of him dying in the den toyed with her mind until she scrambled to her feet and ran for the exit. "Oren!" she cried.

"Nahtaia!" Kale hissed. "Calm down! Haven't you ever had a cold before?"

She whipped around and shook her head. "Faeries don't get sick. Poisoned, sure, but not sick."

He stood up and something in his air changed. He wobbled and looked like he was about to explode. Nahtaia didn't know if he actually would. She watched as he ran past her and dropped to his hands and knees on the branch and wretched.

"Oren!" she shrieked, not knowing what to do. "Oren!"

Oren sped toward them, panic-stricken. Nahtaia gestured to Kale with her other hand on her heaving chest, and a look of realization came over his features. He smirked. "By the Highest Power, Nahtaia," he said, rubbing his hands down his face. "With your overreacting, someone would think you were being pecked to death by an owl."

Nahtaia suddenly flung herself at him and buried her face in his shoulder.

"Never mind. Panic on," he said in approval.

"What's wrong with him?" she whined. "Is he dying?"

Oren looked over his shoulder at Kale, who'd just finished his episode. "He looks sick."

"Well, obviously!" she barked, shoving away from him.

He laughed and invitingly opened his arms. "Vomiting is the sign of his final moments in life," he said, almost mournfully.

"Not funny!" she snapped.

"I'm better already," Kale groaned as he passed the pair. Nahtaia turned and followed after him.

"Are you sure?" she asked. "What do you need to make you better?"

"Rest," he and Oren replied in unison. Oren turned back and went to gather some food.

The rain went on for most of the day, and when it finally came to an end, Dweegen was waiting for the trio at the bottom of the tree. Kale was still feverish but did seem to regain some color in his face. When the earthmover heard of their little "ill adventure," he hurried home, then returned with some medicine. It quickly took effect, and Kale was back to normal when they met their ride toward the Willow of D'Irdda.

The underground area where they stood was wide and tall, thus deeper under the earth. Earthmovers abounded, loitering in conversation with one another or bargaining with food and clothing from the packs each wore on their back. Saddled rats stood at the entrances to three of the five tunnels that snaked off of the large area.

Dweegen waddled over to a brown and white rat, the largest of the three with the widest saddle, and exchanged words with the earthmover who stood with it. The man quickly looked up to the three with a glint of wonder in his eyes. He nodded, and Dweegen motioned for the three to come forward.

"This is Snippet," Dweegen said, gesturing to the rat. The animal squeaked at the mention of its name. "She will take you to the border of Gaia Faults, but no farther. With the magic barrier around the elven territory, these rats cannot enter."

A smile spread on Oren's face and he glanced down at Nahtaia. "Gaia Faults is perfect. Thank you for all your help."

"Yes, thank you," Nahtaia and Kale echoed.

"Thank you for the, um, adventure," Dweegen replied, though it was more than obvious how pleased he was to get rid of the "unfortunate" group.

Oren mounted first, then held his hand out for Nahtaia. She stared at his hand then looked to Kale, eyebrows lifted.

"How, exactly, are we going about this?" she asked the men.

"You sit in front of me," they both replied.

They all exchanged awkward glances. "Never mind," she said with a shake of her head and mounted behind Oren. "I'm staying in *between* the two of you."

"Understand this," Dweegen started. "Gaia Faults is still very far from here. I'm not sure when the last traveler went to or came from there. Snippet will make stops at marked areas to regain strength, find food, and recoup. Please be patient with her."

The trio nodded, and with a final goodbye, the rat jerked forward. Nahtaia tightened her hold around Oren and Kale did the same to her as the journey began.

Snippet ran surprisingly fast. They sped through so quickly, the walls of the tunnel seemed a blur and Nahtaia wondered just how long it would take to reach the Faults.

Oren looked down at Nahtaia's hands around him and covered them with one of his own.

"I never quite realized how tiny you actually are, Nahtaia," he called over his shoulder.

Nahtaia grit her teeth and blushed when he looked over his shoulder with a dimpled grin. She tried to avoid his eyes and turned her gaze to Kale. A slight smile on his face brought a wider smile to her own.

"What?" she laughed.

"I never imagined I'd be riding a giant rat, underground, with a couple of faeries," he replied. "It's odd."

Oren's back tensed. "I never imagined a human could be so irritating," he retorted, then howled in pain. He whipped his head around and looked wide-eyed at Nahtaia. "Did you just bite me?"

She poked out her tongue and fought the smile that tried to surface.

Chapter 14

The underground atmosphere veiled the passing of time. There was no way to know just how long one sped beneath the earthy surface. The muddy walls were so dark they were almost non-existent and seemed never-ending, going on and on without a light at the end of the tunnel.

The rat was quick and strong. Her muscles worked hard under the weight of the faeries and human, but she seemed to be used to that sort of travel.

Seven stops were made underground, three of them being what Nahtaia assumed were night-long rests. The idea of traveling for so long with no sunlight created a sense of claustrophobia within her, so she spent much of the ride trying to keep her eyes downcast.

At one point, Nahtaia fell asleep with her cheek against Oren, who didn't seem to mind.

A strange smell, like lavender and herbs, grew stronger the farther they traveled through the tunnel. Kale looked to Oren, who was focused intently on the ceiling of the tunnel. He looked up and saw roots weaving in and out of the dirt. Still at a full run, Snippet darted left to dodge a hanging root. Nahtaia shifted to the side and nearly fell off the rat, but Kale grabbed her before she was lost.

She shot up with a gasp and gripped Oren just before Snippet dodged another root and the three shifted to the other side.

"What's going on?" Nahtaia asked. Her heart beat so fast her head was spinning.

Oren looked over his shoulder at the pair and concern creased his brow. "It looks like a rough ride up ahead."

Nahtaia and Kale leaned to the side to see what he meant by that and they all tensed. A forest of hanging tree roots created a labyrinth of dirt and wood, threatening a bash to the head of anyone caught unaware.

Snippet leaned, ducked, swerved, and leaped through the obstacles. The riders could do nothing but hold on, hoping to not get snagged on something along the way.

"Dweegen forgot to mention this part," Kale called.

"Or he knew and thought it was bad fortune to tell us," Nahtaia retorted. "That rat."

Snippet huffed at the remark and Nahtaia uttered an apology.

The lavender scent overwhelmed the herbal one and Kale leaned in so Nahtaia could hear him better when he asked, "What's that smell?"

Nahtaia looked up at the roots and turned her head with a smile. "Dryads," she replied.

Kale's brows lifted in surprise. "I've never seen a dryad before."

"Oh no," Oren said as Snippet slowed to a walk. Nahtaia looked ahead over his shoulder and saw the tunnel was obscured. Poor Snippet walked up to the dirt and pat it with her paws. After a sniff and a squeak of displeasure, the three realized there was no way through.

"No!" Nahtaia cried, climbing off the rat. "No. This can't be possible." She started to dig in the dirt while the men looked on.

"Nahtaia," Oren started.

"No, I won't accept this," she squealed. "There has to be a way through. We're so close. I know we are." She raked at the dirt with her nails as the others just watched. "Don't move like snails *now*! Help me dig."

Kale dropped from the rat. "Nahtaia, we should just go—"

"I'm not going back," she snapped. "We've been riding for *days*."

Oren studied the tunnel as Kale joined Nahtaia in what seemed like a futile move to dig, when he took an arrow from his quiver. He jumped down from Snippet, landing nimbly on his feet, then stuck the arrow into the walls and ceiling of the tunnel. Nahtaia looked up at him and frowned.

"What are you doing?" she asked.

He continued to stab the dirt in numerous places when, in one spot, the arrow slid through with no effort.

The dirt around it crumbled to the floor. Oren looked down at Nahtaia with a grin and she shot to her feet.

"You're brilliant!" she cried.

The three, along with Snippet, started to dig through the dirt and soon found it getting warmer.

"I think we're getting close," Kale said, and Snippet squeaked in agreement.

Daylight broke through when the last layers of dirt fell from their fingers, and they all eagerly climbed out. Nahtaia blocked the sun from her eyes as she looked overhead in awe. The willow was still many miles away, but even so, its size was overwhelming.

She started her way toward the tree, but Oren stepped in front of her. "Whoa, whoa, whoa. I think it would be a good time to rest," he suggested. "Snippet needs it."

Nahtaia looked back at the rat and smiled sweetly. "Snippet, you're free to go to your family," she said, then pushed past Oren.

"No, wait!" Oren groaned. "She can still take us the rest of the way, but she needs rest."

"We can't keep stopping. We'll never get anywhere!"

Kale ran up beside her and tried to reason with her. "We're all tired, Nahtaia. We need rest."

"Even if we do go now, it'll still be a few days' run there with Snippet," Oren explained. "Without her, it'll be twice as long."

She thought about that for a moment before dropping down onto her bottom with a sigh. "Why does this whole trip have to take so long?"

Oren whispered something to Snippet and she ran off with a nod. He turned back to Nahtaia and Kale and said, "We can sleep the night and start again before first light. Snippet will find a suitable shelter."

The three sat in silence, basking in the warmth of the sun. Rain clouds melted in the distance and the resulting cool breeze was comforting.

Kale smiled and let out a laugh. The faeries looked at him quizzically.

"I'm sorry," he said. "But have you looked at us?"

Nahtaia and Oren glanced at themselves with a laugh. They were covered in dirt from head to toe.

"All right," Nahtaia said, rising to her feet. "Next plan. I'm going to find some water and get cleaned up."

Oren stood up and replied, "All right, but I'm coming too."

Nahtaia froze and eyed him. "Only to keep the birds at bay, but when we find water, I'm on my own."

Oren smiled with a quiet "of course," then winked at Kale, who shook his head with a sigh.

By nightfall, things were not so bad. Snippet actually *made* them a shelter beneath a tree where the cold was blocked by the rat's fur. Everyone was clean. Everyone was fed. Everyone slept comfortably. If all were to keep going so well, then the remainder of the journey didn't seem so bad to Nahtaia.

Two mornings after, as soon as everyone was up, they were on their way toward Gaia Faults. Hopes and moods were high and smiles were in abundance. By late afternoon, they were but half a mile from their destination, which meant Snippet couldn't go much farther. Oren was on alert, trying to sense a change in the magic in the air, so as not to run straight into the invisible barrier.

"So, do you even have in mind what you're going to say to a Voice?" Kale asked Nahtaia.

She sighed and bit her lip in thought. "The truth, I suppose," she replied. "I'll have something worked out by then."

Snippet came to an abrupt stop and Nahtaia screamed as the three jerked forward, nearly tumbling off the edge of a thirty-foot cliff. Rushing waters roared below—she couldn't even imagine the terrifying fall if Snippet hadn't stopped in time. They climbed off the rat and looked over the edge, confused and speechless. Well, the men were speechless.

"Since when was there a *river* this near to the elves?" she shrieked. "Is this a joke? That earthmover said Snippet could take us to the Faults!"

"Maybe we'd have gone under the river if the tunnel wasn't blocked," Kale said.

Nahtaia looked into the distance on either side for a bridge or any other way to cross on foot. Oren turned to Snippet and sighed. "I guess this is it, girl," he said, patting her on the head. "You've been a great help." Snippet's attention bounced between Oren, Kale, and

Nahtaia before she nodded and turned. The three called their thanks and returned their focus to the river.

"I guess we fly over," Oren sighed. "It's not far." Without another word, he took Kale by the wrists and lifted him off the ground. Kale held his breath as the immensity of height and power of the water almost seemed to mock his small size. Oren was right about it not being far and he was soon dropped in the grass on the other side.

Nahtaia watched from the other side as they spent a few moments in what seemed like mellow conversation. "What in the world could they possibly have to say to each other right now?" she wondered. When they both looked toward her, she knew they were discussing her. Nahtaia waved a hand, telling Oren to hurry to up and come back to take her across.

"What were you two talking about?" she snipped when he landed in front of her.

He glanced once over his shoulder, then back at Nahtaia and said, "I think we've finally come to an agreement."

Chapter 15

Terry sat by the window, watching droplets of water run down the glass. Her brother was out there somewhere and a storm was coming. A big one. The town was in an uproar earlier in the day when the morning was dark and the sky in the distance was as black as poison. The people wiped the markets clean of food and wood for fire; they even boarded up their windows. Even in that moment, as Terry's eyes were glazed in thoughts far away, lightening streaked the skies and thunder rumbled through the earth.

More than a week had passed since Kale had gone missing.

Grandmama was in the main room, baking some cookies for comfort. It was the only method she had to soothe the nerves of everyone in the house. The search for Kale had been called off two days earlier and townspeople began talking. Some were sure Kale had been charmed to death while others, like Grandfather, still hoped for his return.

"He's a smart boy," he would say. "He knows his way home."

Grandmama wasn't so positive. She blamed herself for their grandson's death. She insulted the fae and this was their revenge.

By the time Grandfather was done boarding windows and cutting firewood, the heavens poured rain as if the sea was above.

"If the faeries didn't kill Kale," Grandmama said with a croak, "this storm surely will."

Grandfather slammed the door shut behind him. "Don't start with this again," he growled. "Have some faith in the boy. He deserves more credit than this."

"Where's Willy?" Terry asked, her eyes glued to the sky.

"He's in his room," Grandmama replied. "He was asleep the last time I checked. I think he's fallen ill."

Light flashed across the room, followed by a loud crash of thunder. Everyone gasped in surprise, and Grandmama's hand rested on her heart.

"Hopefully Willy won't be in need of a doctor anytime soon," Grandfather sighed.

What kind of agreement could Oren and Kale ever come to? Nahtaia thought. Again.

It was the one thought that nagged her as they walked through the fields toward the outstretched fingers of the Willow of D'Irdda. Kale kept his eyes ahead while Oren continually looked up at the sky behind them. Neither said any more on whatever they "agreed" upon before, and Nahtaia was losing her patience. She looked sidelong at Kale through her hair that fell like a screen between then. He seemed content. No emotion showed on his face. She frowned at his bland behavior and looked back at Oren. He flashed her a grin and she grit her teeth in response.

"How are you, Bluebird?" he asked when she looked forward again.

She didn't look at him when she replied, "I'm fine." She looked over her shoulder and saw him looking over his own.

"What do you keep looking at?" she asked. At that, Kale finally looked up and followed her gaze. Oren turned toward her, biting his lip in thought.

"You don't by any chance feel something in the air, do you?" Oren asked. "A storm, perhaps."

Nahtaia spotted the clouds and frowned. "I don't feel anything, but it smells like rain," she said.

Not a moment later, a distant rumble of thunder made the three look back all at once. Worry was etched on Oren's face. "I really think this is a serious storm," he said, running a hand through his hair. "We should find somewhere high to settle."

"Settle? We hardly left," Nahtaia whined. "Do we plan on ever making it to the elves? Because at this rate—"

"We will make it to them," Oren cut in. "But I'd like to make it alive rather than as a half-drowned fool who couldn't hang up the journey for a bit when the rains came."

Nahtaia planted her hands on her hips with a glare. "I don't like the way you're talking to me."

"I thought you'd have been used to it by now," Kale interjected smugly.

Oren flashed his teeth in a grin that irked Nahtaia. She glanced between the pair and her nostrils flared in annoyance.

"Okay, that's it. I demand to know what it is you two agreed on."

Kale dropped his gaze back to the ground, but his smile didn't fade. He shook his head, about to shrug off the request, but Oren blurted, "He's given up."

Kale snapped to attention and Nahtaia lifted her eyebrows in confusion. "What?" she said.

"Oren, you could stand to be a *little* more—" Kale started, as a blush overtook his cheeks.

"It's the truth," Oren interrupted.

Nahtaia turned to Kale. "Given up? What does that mean?"

"Look, I just don't see—"

"He's finally accepted that he can't have you," Oren explained.

With that, silence fell over the group. Kale interested himself in a brown leaf on the ground. Oren stared at Nahtaia with a smile and Nahtaia pressed her lips in thought. A crow cawed and a sudden breeze blew some pieces of hair into her face.

"So," she started with a stutter. "S-so, you just stopped caring? Just l-like that?"

Kale slowly shook his head, his eyes still downcast. "I didn't stop caring. I just don't—"

Oren laughed and squeezed her shoulders. "Does it matter, Bluebird?"

She jerked away from him. "Well, it kind of makes me wonder."

"It *doesn't* matter," Kale said. "You're in love with Oren."

That was not what Nahtaia was expecting. She took a step back, shock twisting her face. "Excuse me?" she squealed. "I am not!"

"Oh please," Kale chuckled as he stepped past her and continued toward the Faults. "It's been obvious since the first time he appeared. It's only a matter of time until you realize and accept it yourself."

"There is nothing to realize and nothing to accept!" she shouted. "I don't know what has gotten into you two, but I will not stand for this! I am not in love with anyone, let alone the selfish, Dweegen-loving Oren!"

Oren frowned and cocked his head to the side. "Dweegen-loving?"

"Oh, shut it. I'm running out of insults." She hurried to keep alongside Kale as she continued her rant. "He has been there my entire life either getting me in trouble or getting me angry. Usually both."

Oren scoffed. "I've never gotten you in trouble."

"And haven't you seen all of the anger and, and, and, and tension and arguments between him and me? Where would 'love' come in with any of that? Hmm? The very thought is absurd."

Kale whipped around and Nahtaia could tell that he was trying to fight a smile.

"You know what I saw, Nahtaia?" he said. "I saw you look to him whenever we've been in trouble. I saw you lose the fire in your eyes when you thought he was dead."

"Not to mention your reaction to our kiss, Bluebird," Oren added.

Her eyes widened as she marched right up to Oren, her face just three inches from his, poking him quite violently in the chest. "That was you using magic on me! I was charmed!"

He took her finger in his hand with a squeeze, then leaned down to her and said, "I did nothing but touch my lips to yours."

She searched his eyes for a glint of deception; a hint of him speaking a lie or hiding that he did, in fact, charm her. When she saw nothing, she yanked her finger from him, turned, and stomped on her way.

"Great," Kale sighed.

Not five minutes later, Nahtaia's dramatic show came to a halt, as did the journey. She walked straight into an invisible wall. Rubbing her painful, pounding nose, she put her hand up to feel what she ran into. It was invisible but a glow of magic emanated under every touch.

Oren's hand came up beside hers but went right through the wall that hindered her. She looked up at him with panic in her eyes as he walked past her on the other side.

"It's the elven barrier," he said. "I didn't realize it was so far from the willows."

Nahtaia ran her hands over the barrier, then pounded on it, trying to break through or find a weak spot. "No, no, no," she said in a feeble cry.

Kale then stood beside Oren on the other side. Nahtaia threw her hands to her head.

"You can't pass. You've been banned," Oren said.

It took Nahtaia a moment to react.

"No, no, no, no, no," she cried, covering her face. "This was all a waste of time. Thinking I could fix things; thinking I could somehow get to the elves." She wiped her tears on her arm and shook her head. "I was so hopeful."

"It's still possible," Kale said. "We can—"

"No. None of it ever was. Oren, you said so yourself. 'No one just goes to the Voices.' It's hopeless."

"Nahtaia, I never thought you'd even make it so far out of Lyra without wings," Oren said. "You've already done more than I conceived was possible."

Nahtaia dropped to her bottom and stared at the grass as it swayed in the cool air. She didn't know how much time had passed since they'd left Kale's farm. It couldn't have been a month, since another full moon had not yet come. However long it was, it was all useless. Pointless traveling and fighting off nature. Weathering storms and arguing with the men about love and kisses and feelings. All of it, ridiculous.

Thunder rumbled above.

"We should get back to the trees," Oren said, scanning the sky. "And fast."

A flock of birds scattered into the air at a sudden flash of lightning. Normally, the faeries would worry about birds, but this time, even the faery-eating creatures were fleeing for their lives; they weren't interested in finding food.

"I'll go find somewhere for us to stay." The second Oren finished speaking, he immediately flew out of sight.

Kale was about to hurry in the same direction but froze when Nahtaia didn't move. "I took the concern in Oren's voice seriously enough; why aren't you?" he asked as he looked up toward the trees, then back at Nahtaia on the ground. "Nahtaia, we have to go."

She didn't respond. Kale took her hand and urged her to move, but instead, she just looked at his hand, then lifted her eyes to his.

"Kiss me," she said.

Kale wrinkled his forehead and swallowed. "What?"

"I need to know what I feel," she continued.

His heart suddenly pounded. "What do you mean?"

"I mean, a part of me is disappointed that you gave up, and I don't understand."

Kale gazed at her in wonder and felt heat rise to his face. "I'm not kissing you, Nahtaia. We need to go. Your mind is in the wrong place right now."

"Is it? What else is there to think about? I've failed us. I've ruined you." Nahtaia looked down at her hands. "I'm sorry," she whispered.

Kale lifted her chin and smiled. "We'll find a way. Without the Voices." He wiped away the one tear that managed to fall from her eye and helped her to her feet. "They're not the only beings of magic in all of Jaydür; even I know that."

Nahtaia nodded, though she wasn't feeling much better. Only so many options lay before them, and most of them included returning to Lyra. The very thought terrified her.

Without another word, Nahtaia and Kale started their walk back toward the forest, and with another rumble of thunder, rain began to fall.

Back in Lyra, the faeries gathered in a hollowed-out tree known as the Community Oak. Rain drummed on the wood above them.

Minister Moriel stood with the other city leaders around a desk in a private room. Ministers Sentinian, Groblen, and Astoun were all present, and each was in deep thought. It took the faeries of Lyra nearly three days to realize that Nahtaia and Oren had disappeared. When humans filled the forest calling out a name, obviously searching for someone, Moriel instinctively knew the missing person had something to do with the missing faeries.

"Death or exile are the only options," Astoun said with a sigh. Her delicate fingers tapped her plump red lips in rhythm with the rain.

"I think death would only be appropriate if she'd killed someone," Sentinian added.

Moriel was tired of the conversation by then. An hour of listening to the ministers argue was more daunting than one would think. He smoothed his white hair away from his face and looked up to his colorful audience. Astoun's wild red hair—the trademark of the fire fae—was like a flame in the dim light. Sentinian's bright lilac eyes were darker than most flower faes', and Groblen's green lips were a reminder to all (especially Lyra's young ladies) of their missing military leader, Oren. Each minister had something to say—a piece of advice to give—but Moriel did not have the patience to listen any longer.

He rose from his chair. "Pardon my leave, but I am in desperate need of quiet."

"But what do we do until the storm passes?" Sentinian asked.

A crash of thunder shook the oak down to its roots.

Moriel looked up and shook his head. "I think we have plenty of time."

"And this time should be used most diligently," a fifth voice radiated through the tree in a light, ethereal timbre. The ministers spun in circles, wondering where the voice came from. "Even more so in a situation such as this, Minister Moriel," the voice went on.

Moriel looked to the ministers. As if they all had the same thought at the same time, each rushed to the main entrance of the oak tree, just feet from the ground.

"Open the door," Moriel ordered the men standing guard. They immediately did as they were told. Wood groaned against wood as they lifted a crossbar, then pushed open the door. The ministers flew out into the rain and found a human-sized woman standing at the tree. They exchanged awed glances, then Moriel flew up to look the woman in the face.

Moriel's stresses washed away as bright yellow eyes bore into his. Golden spirals of hair framed a glowing face sprinkled with freckles. He immediately knew who she was.

"Poette," Moriel bowed his head. "Great Voice of Mae'Ehr, to what does my city owe the honor of your visit?"

Poette's eyes squinted with her graceful smile. "'To whom' is the question, dear minister," she laughed. Her ethereal voice rang like wind chimes in a soft breeze. "And my answer?" She raised one finger before Moriel and said, "One little faery who has caught my attention. She has made me laugh, cry, and respect my sister Voices for the control they hold over their tongues. Minister Moriel, you have a fierce little moon faery on your hands, and my sisters and I have come to love her dearly."

Chapter 16

Nahtaia, Oren, and Kale did not find a shelter by the time the rains arrived. At the very least, the storm did not come in an instantaneous downpour as it had in the past. Water trickled down through the leaves and branches as the trio wandered the forest floor. Oren would occasionally fly up into the canopy in search of an empty den—as there were usually many—but came back with a frown-tugged face every time.

Kale kept his eyes on the road before them, skimming the expanse of trees and shrubs for enemy critters or birds.

Nahtaia, on the other hand, was lost in utter confusion with herself. A sense of defeat overwhelmed her now that she knew she could not cross into the elven territory. She had dragged Oren and Kale for days on end, convinced she was going to fix things. She always fixed things—until now. Her mind and heart were a mess.

The only sound in the forest was that of crunching leaves beneath the feet of the travelers. All creatures were snuggled away in their homes, weathering out the storm. A chill breeze began to blow and Nahtaia looked up to Kale. After his feverish episode not too long before, she was overly careful about the human's fragility in the weather.

"We need to get you somewhere warm," she said.

Kale turned to her but Oren interrupted before he could speak.

"You don't have to play strong, Bluebird," he said.

Nahtaia wrapped her arms around herself. She hoped it wasn't so obvious that she was frozen to the bone. "I'm fine," she whispered in reply. "*I* won't get sick. *He* will."

Oren ground his teeth and flew back up into the canopy. Kale touched the small of her back and she flashed him a plastic smile. "I'm fine," she said. "Really."

It took Oren but a moment to return with a sense of relief washing over his features. "There's a nest up there," he said. "It looks like it was abandoned days ago. We'll still get wet but we'll be off the ground."

After a quick agreement, Nahtaia wrapped her arms around Oren's neck as he flew her up to the nest. A familiar scent made her skin ripple—his woodsy breath. Only it wasn't just his breath after all. It was his skin and his hair, too. Everything about him.

Oh no, she thought, suddenly aware of his hands brushing her bare skin at her back. Her heart sped as she closed her eyes and took a deep breath.

Oren pulled his face back and looked down at her curiously. "Are you all right?"

She opened her eyes and found him staring down at her, close enough to make her blush. "Yes," she replied. She licked her lips, which had suddenly become dry, and looked away. "Just put me down."

It was hard to miss the twitch of his mouth as he fought a smile.

Kale was soon dropped into the nest alongside Nahtaia while Oren went off on yet another search for a den. The rains fell harder.

"We're not going to be safe here," Nahtaia said, studying the intricately woven nest. "It's strong but not strong enough."

Kale looked over the edge of the nest and frowned at the distance between them and the ground. "I'm sure Oren will find something." He slumped down onto the ground and furrowed his brow. "Nahtaia," he sighed. "Do you feel as useless as I do?"

She turned to him and frowned. She knew what he was trying to say. Oren seemed to be doing all the work in the world for them. By all means, this was not a new realization, but it was hitting Nahtaia harder than usual. She was exhausted. Kale looked exhausted. But Oren kept going, always staying strong and keeping his head on his shoulders, never losing sight of what needed to be done.

Dropping down beside Kale, Nahtaia let out a small smile. "Yes. I feel beyond useless. If I had my wings, at the very least, we could have flown you with us. I'd be helping in the search for shelter and a trip like this probably would have been over three days ago."

Kale chuckled. "Convenience is such a difficult thing to come across, it seems."

"Apparently."

The two sat in silence for a moment before Nahtaia looked up and asked, "What are you going to do when you get back home?"

Kale thought for a moment, then turned his face to the dark sky above them. "Find a new job, I guess."

"Start a new statue?"

He looked down at her and smirked. "If that man ever took the last one. How about you?"

Nahtaia dropped her gaze and fiddled with a twig that was half woven into the nest. "I don't know what I'm going to do. I doubt the ministers will allow me entry back into the city if they've realized my absence."

At that, Kale stiffened and sat up, turning to look her in the face. "What do you mean?"

Nahtaia eyed him with a frown.

"They have to let you go back home," he prodded.

"No, they don't. What I've done gives me no right to the city or the people. But as I've just said, that's *if* they find out what I've done." Nahtaia smoothed her hair from her face with a sigh. "If they haven't realized, and I somehow manage to get my wings and magic back, then I will try to find a suitable assignment to keep me busy and out of trouble."

Kale pulled his knees to his chest and wrapped his arms around them. "Assignment?"

"A job. Something that will help the city, the people. Watching for enemies, cleaning the forest, gathering food. Things like that."

Something above Nahtaia's head caught Kale's eye, and he climbed to his feet with a squint. Nahtaia followed his gaze.

"What is it?" she asked.

He pointed his finger and replied, "Isn't that a den?"

He was right. Just a couple yards above them was a den. It looked big enough. The two climbed up the bark and made their way inside it.

"It's perfect!" Kale laughed. "We can find something to cover the entrance and we'll be fine."

It was larger than any den they'd stayed in before.

"I wonder what animal lived here," Nahtaia said. "Maybe a raccoon?"

"Does it matter?"

"Well, no but—"

"Nahtaia?" Oren's voice echoed through the forest. She looked down from the den and couldn't help but smile at the look of panic on his face. "Nahtaia!" he cried out once more.

She lay on her belly and called out to him. "Hey, birdbrain." He looked up and let out a breath of relief.

"What are you doing up there?" he asked as he flew to her, hovering face-to-face with her.

"Kale spotted it," she said, blushing at his closeness. A smile pulled at her lips.

As if he wasn't close enough already, he leaned in even more and smiled his charming half-smile. "Does that make it better than the one I just found?"

"Jealous?" Kale asked from behind Nahtaia. She sat up and let her legs hang over the edge.

"No," Oren smirked. "But the one I found won't be having any visitors tonight."

Nahtaia looked to Kale, who frowned at Oren. "What do you mean?" he asked. Oren pointed down the tree, and Nahtaia and Kale hurried to the edge to see. A bushbear climbed the trunk, blinking against the rain pelting its face.

Nahtaia gave Kale a sympathetic smile. "You tried," she said.

He shook his head and sighed.

When the three were finally settled in the new den, the storm blew in with great force. Oren had already gathered food and constructed a cover for the door with twigs, vines, and leaves, leaving Nahtaia and Kale quite impressed.

"You can do just about anything," Nahtaia muttered as she studied the makeshift door.

"Do you use anything to make it stick?" Kale asked, coming up beside her.

Oren shook his head. "The woods are wet, and wet, living wood bends whereas dry or dead wood doesn't. With a tight enough weave, there's no need for anything sticky."

Nahtaia knew as much, as all fae had the basic knowledge of how to build shelters, but Oren's craftsmanship was something else. She never quite paid much attention to Oren's handiwork, but looking at it now, his skill was comparable to Kale's statue-carving skill. Not only would the door hold, it was so tightly woven that not even light would spill through the cracks, let alone rain.

Nahtaia looked over her shoulder at Oren, who wasn't paying attention to her. She was impressed by his workmanship.

Kale and Oren ate in silence, ignoring each other for the most part. Nahtaia didn't mind. It was better than them fighting.

The wind outside howled through the trees and shook the one the three rested in. Lightning crashed so frequently that Nahtaia was almost always aware of where the men lay. She couldn't imagine being out there in such a storm. It would have washed them away, no doubt.

Kale curled up against the wall of the den, though Nahtaia wasn't sure whether he was actually sleeping or not. Oren was on his stomach, fluttering his wings in rhythm with a song he hummed.

Nahtaia found herself staring at him, and with every passing hour, her thoughts raced through all he'd risked over the time they were out in the woods. For a man who sacrificed so much, he seemed the most at peace.

Nahtaia knew she was seen as a chaotic creature, always getting into trouble and causing stress for everyone around her. But not Oren. Yet here he was.

Guilt ate her up inside. What had she done to deserve his time and attention besides giving him trouble and making accusations? That was it; she didn't deserve him.

After hours of rain and lightning crashes turned to rumbling thunder, silence grew thick within the den. Oren's humming eventually stopped and turned to steady breathing. Kale's face was smoothed in slumber and his eyes shifted rapidly beneath his eyelids. He was likely reliving some of the absurd events that had taken place during their journey.

Nahtaia slowly, quietly walked to the door and pushed it open, just slightly, spilling a scant amount of white moonlight into the darkness of the den. Rain still fell, but it was quiet and gentle. The moon hung behind a thinning veil of clouds. She breathed in the fresh scent of wet dirt and wood, and pangs of homesickness turned her stomach. Nahtaia wanted to go *home.*

With a swallow, she turned and made her way to Kale. Muscles in his face twitched and she couldn't help but smile. Oren shifted behind her, and even in the faded moonlight, she could see that he'd rolled onto his back. He was still sleeping, his chest rising and falling with each breath. His eyes remained still and his lips…

She looked away when she caught herself admiring every detail of his face. It was expected, Nahtaia knew, but it was not something she thought she would ever do. It *was* Oren, after all. The man who'd driven her crazy for much of her life. The man who always happened to be around when she was in trouble. The man who brought out the strangest feelings with something as simple as a kiss.

"Curse you, Nahtaia," she whispered to herself. *Get a hold of yourself. He charmed you, remember?* She couldn't believe what was swimming in her mind.

But, she thought as her eyes drifted once more to him, *he claims he did no such thing.* Blood rushed to her head with anxiety and curiosity. He was sleeping. Kale was sleeping. Now was the best time to find out whether or not Oren really had charmed her.

Before she could think twice on the idea, she was already kneeling beside him, tucking her hair behind her ears. She licked her lips and stared at his.

You're mad, Nahtaia, she thought. *Mad as an eastern dwarf. What if he wakes up?* She closed her eyes and responded to her conscience. *I'll tell him the truth. It's not like he'd disapprove anyway.*

With her heart pounding, she gathered her hair to one side so it wouldn't fall in his face and wake him before she could get the truth about him. Her blood was cold in her trembling hands. She swallowed a knot in her throat and with her eyes closed, leaned down to Oren.

Her lips were so close that she could feel his breath on her. She thought for a millisecond about pulling back but lightly kissed him before she acted on it. It was just a touch, but he woke up.

Oren let out a subtle gasp of surprise and blinked away his sleep. When he realized it was Nahtaia and what she was doing, it took him but a breath to take advantage of the moment. With a hand on the back of her head, he gently pulled her in for another kiss. His breaths came rapidly when her hands cupped his face, and she *didn't* pull away.

Her heart throbbed. Her mind spun. Nahtaia's hands ran over his jaw then down his arms, touching every dip and ridge of his skin and muscles. Whatever was happening, she wasn't sure she wanted it to end. It was as if all of her troubles and worries and hardships were suddenly being shared. Half of all that she'd been through was lifted off of her shoulders. A sense of relief and familiarity overcame her, and she suddenly understood it; the rush, the heat and the cold, and the open pores—it all washed over her and this time, she knew she wasn't being charmed. This time, she could see, finally, that Oren felt like *home.*

Oren drove his fingers through her hair and she basked in the sense of desire that came from him. It was raw and needy and strong all at the same time. His lips were warm and sweet but it was the smell of his skin and breath that kept her there. It reminded her of Lyra and the comforts she missed so deeply, which *did* make sense in the end. Oren knew her. Nahtaia knew him.

It was only when she was lightheaded and out of breath that she pulled away from Oren. With his hand on the back of her neck, he kept her from going too far, pressing his forehead against hers. Nahtaia opened her eyes and looked up at him through her lashes.

"Finally," he whispered.

Nahtaia dropped her gaze with a shaky sigh. "I'm so confused."

Oren laughed and kissed her again. "It's not that difficult to understand, Bluebird."

She dropped her eyes to the ground while Oren ran a thumb over her lips. Everything was going to change. Life was going to be different. She could feel it already beginning, and part of her wondered if she secretly wanted it all along.

No. This is definitely new, she thought. She was drawn from her thoughts when Oren dipped in for another kiss. Kale rolled over in his sleep and Nahtaia quickly pulled away, eyeing his body on the ground with her hand on her heart.

"Relax, Nahtaia," Oren chuckled.

"Don't tell Kale," she whispered in reply.

"It's not a big deal. What are you trying to hide?"

Her eyes bore into Oren's. "Just don't tell him," she begged. "I don't want to hurt him anymore. Please, Oren."

He nodded sympathetically, then took her hand and brought it to his lips. "I won't tell him."

Chapter 17

After the rain, the forest was refreshed from the roots of every tree to the branches at the tip of the canopy. Moisture glistened off rocks and leaves and made the ground cool and soft to walk on. Life in the forest sprang up with new fervor, but most of all, Oren's ego was brightened. Nahtaia wasn't sure she was ready for that.

Every thirty seconds, he'd look over at her with that dimple-dipping smile. He'd brush up against her every time he had an opportunity or he'd stealthily give her hand a squeeze. Her heart pounded every time but not out of excitement; it was out of fear of Kale noticing.

For Nahtaia, not much really *had* changed other than the way she saw Oren. Her situation was still just as hopeless as it was the day before. She couldn't make it to the elves. Her plan was worthless and a waste of time, and as the three stood before the elven barrier once again, all of the negatives upset her all over again. She stared at the glowing magic around her hand as she pushed it against the barrier.

"We should go," Oren said, looking over and through the barrier.

Kale turned with a frown. "Go where?"

"Back to Lyra. It's the only chance we still have."

Nahtaia thought momentarily on the kiss the night before. It almost made her believe she still had the slightest bit of magic within her, but in that moment, at the mention of returning to Lyra, it seeped away through every pore of her being. She was magicless. And hopeless.

"I dragged you two with me. I put you through so much danger and trouble." She paused to steady her breaking voice. "For nothing."

Oren put a hand on one shoulder as Kale put his on the other.

"It wasn't for nothing," Oren said.

"I wouldn't change this journey if I had the chance," Kale added.

"What do you mean?" Nahtaia moaned, leaning her back against the barrier. "All you got from this was being shrunk, dragged around, sick, pushed around by Oren, and—"

"And even so," Kale interrupted, "no other human being can brag as much as I can now."

Nahtaia looked up at him with a frown. Oren's eyebrows pinched together in curiosity.

"We humans wait for a story. We wait for something worthy of sharing with our family and friends. Something that will keep us in high regard in the eyes of those around us. And this," he motioned with his hands to their surroundings. "This is incredible. No other human will have a story like mine, Nahtaia. I wouldn't trade it for the world."

Eyes brimming with tears, Nahtaia let herself slide down the barrier, but before her bottom touched the ground, Oren slid his arm around her waist and pulled her along.

"No," he said. "We'll have none of that. We're going back to Lyra."

Oren tried to change the subject, but Nahtaia was thinking hard on what Kale just admitted. She turned in one swift move and leaped into Kale's arms, wrapping her own tightly around his neck.

"Thank you," she whispered. He rubbed one hand gently on her back while trying to ignore Oren's huffing and puffing.

Kale replied, "There's nothing to thank me for."

The journey turned back to the woods; back to the same trail that had taken them to what they had believed was Nahtaia's best chance at redemption and Kale's best chance of restoration. Dread hovered over the heads of the three. No one spoke for a while and Nahtaia had withdrawn into her own thoughts.

What would Moriel say? Would he really go so far as to execute her for all the trouble she caused? He'd threatened it in the past and this problem was by far the worst in her lifetime. She was a troublemaker, a hindrance to the city and its people. She couldn't expect to be accepted any longer.

Oren noticed her withdrawal and slowed to walk in step beside her. She let out a subtle gasp at his touch on the small of her back and looked up to meet concerned eyes.

"What is it?" she asked innocently. Kale was far ahead of them, eyeing the canopy and distant forest. Oren slid his hand up to her shoulder and pulled her against him as they walked.

"You're no good at hiding your pain, Bluebird," he said.

"Am I not?" Of course she wasn't. She already knew that. Especially now when she was broken and frail from the stress and disappointment of her failure.

"Everything will be fine," he went on. "One way or another."

But she was not convinced. Of course it would be fine for *him*.

That night, back in a den they previously rested in a few days earlier, they all settled for their sleep. A half-moon was out and Nahtaia excused herself to go bask in the light. She knew she wouldn't feel anything as she did when magic flowed as thickly as the blood in her veins, but still.

Nahtaia frowned when she heard footsteps behind her. "Kale will get suspicious," she said.

"Kale's not as stupid as I thought he was," Oren replied, settling beside her.

"Your first mistake," she countered, trying to lighten her mood. It didn't work.

Oren leaned his elbows on his knees and looked up at the moon through the tree branches. Nahtaia tried to keep her focus on it as well but couldn't with him so close beside her. She never could think straight when it was just the two of them. The moonlight made his green hair look almost white and his skin shone the glow that all creatures of magic held in the light of the moon. His lips pressed in a tight line and she knew he had something to say. He was always outspoken and obnoxious, so why wasn't he saying what he had to say?

"Oren?" she asked, leaning forward to see his face. "What is it?"

He turned with a half-smile. "Nothing."

His lack of confidence in speaking his thoughts was strange and made her suspicious. "Something is obviously wrong," she pressed. "Nothing can possibly get worse than it is. Feel free to say what you need to."

With that, he let out a quiet chuckle. "Nothing is wrong," he said. "I'm just thinking." He gazed at her, his eyes reflected the light around them. There was a flicker of something in them, and after another moment he sighed and said, "You think everything will change."

Nahtaia didn't know what he meant and cocked her head to the side. "What do you mean?"

"I mean *us*."

How strange that a simple, two-letter word could bring a blush to her face and an extra beat to her heart. She looked down at her hands with a small smile. "Everything *will* change," she sighed. "Do you deny it?"

"No, but it won't be a bad change."

He was being too positive. Her shoulders were heavy with the burden of bad thoughts and expectations, and his words were not in agreement with them.

"I won't be allowed back in Lyra," she blurted out. Saying it out loud hurt more than she'd have liked. "I'm going to be executed or banished. I can't expect anything more for all I've done."

Oren ran a hand through his hair with a frown. "What are you saying? Moriel would never do that."

"Oh, please, Oren. You're the one who first warned me."

"Yeah, but I only said it because—"

"Not everything will go your way all the time," Nahtaia went on. Irritation was obvious in her voice, though she didn't mean to make her frustration so clear. "I'm sorry," she said with her hands on her head.

"Moriel listens to me," Oren went on. "I can talk to him. I can work something out."

There he went again. "You don't have to be a hero all the time, Oren. I don't need to be saved from what I deserve."

"What, do you think there's shame in accepting help?"

Nahtaia growled and clawed her fingers down her face in frustration. That wasn't the point. "No," she said through her teeth. "There is no shame in accepting help but—"

"If I can't help you, then I'm coming with you."

She looked at him through her fingers. "What?"

Oren turned his body to look at her full on. "If they banish you, you won't be alone. I think that's the main reason you're so scared. You're afraid to be alone, but you won't be. If they actually banish you, I will come with you."

Frogs croaked in the distance. Nahtaia shook her head. "You're staying in Lyra," she said.

"I've already made my decision," he said with a chuckle.

"You can't leave Lyra. You love Lyra! You live for it! You've dedicated your life to it!"

Oren took her hands and held them firmly against her resisting pull. Leaning in, he looked her straight in the eyes. "If they don't let you stay, they'll have to find someone else to fill my shoes."

Nahtaia shook her head in disbelief. "You're mad."

"Love can drive a man to the edge of the world."

Heart in her throat, Nahtaia felt blood rush through her veins at his words. He noticed the reaction and one side of his lips pulled up as he tucked a bit of her hair behind her ear.

"Don't look so surprised, Bluebird. I've been after you for years. I think I've earned the right to use the word 'love.'"

"Years?" she echoed.

Oren brushed her cheek with his thumb and closed in with a smile. "Years," he said, just before pressing his lips to hers. After one touch, she turned away and put her fingers to her mouth. Kale could easily see them if he was looking. Oren smiled and stood up.

"We'll talk later," he said and made his way inside.

Nahtaia watched Oren walk away and settled her attention on Kale, who curiously studied something above her. Without much more thought, she turned her own face back up to the moon.

Chapter 18

Little Willeim Mason lay limp on the bed. Grandmama dabbed a wet cloth at the sweat that beaded his head. He had been sick since the storm and his fever was still growing. Falling in and out of consciousness, poor Willy had no idea who was with him or what time of day it was.

"We must find a doctor," Terry sniffed, feeling her little brother's suffering deeply. All color had left him, making him pallid as a ghost. A nagging fear repeatedly crept up her spine, whispering thoughts that he wasn't far from becoming the corpse he resembled.

Grandfather grunted and dragged on his pipe. He wouldn't repeat again what he'd said only moments before and more than once. They didn't have the means to pay a doctor and the medication that would heal Willy would surely be costly.

"He'll die," Terry whimpered as she rose to her feet. Her grandfather's cold, hard gaze fell on her, freezing her in her steps.

"Do you think the doctor cares about our Willy?" His voice was deep and gruff. "No one will come within a mile of this place without proof of our ability to pay."

Terry looked down at her little brother and swallowed, holding back the brimming tears. He was trembling.

"If Kale was here, he'd have an answer," she said quietly. The last word was but a croak. Grandmama lifted sad eyes to her granddaughter and shook her head ever so slightly.

"Your brother is gone," she replied. "And I fear he can't come back. That faery took him. Who knows what she's done with him."

Grandmama's face fell back to Willy, and Terry hurried to her room. She paced back and forth, gritting her teeth in frustration.

"He's not dead," she told herself. "Nahtaia wouldn't kill him. She's not evil." She stopped beside her window and pressed her nose against the glass.

"There'd be no need to kill him. With all that magic, killing a human would be pointless." That was when realization sparked somewhere in the deep crevices of her mind, and within moments, that spark blazed into an idea.

Not wasting another second, Terry opened her window and put one leg out before she looked back at the bedroom door.

"My brother is alive," she said aloud as if her words would float to Grandmama's aged ears. "And he's with a cure."

It was strange to be leaving the forest after so much time was taken journeying so deep into it. The trees were constant companions to the three, rising above their heads like towers of a great, never-ending castle. Brown trunks, green leaves, and black stones were all there was to see, and that scene had grown old.

The night passed with much solitude for Nahtaia. The men fell asleep long before it was even a notion for her, especially after Oren's brave declaration.

Love. She thought on the word. It was most definitely not something she ever imagined in the foggy portrait of her future. Then again, Oren was never in that image either. She pondered on the words he'd said the night before.

"I'll go with you," he had said. How could he say something so stupid? His entire life had been planned out since their elementary school years. Being the military hand for Lyra mattered to him ever since he could hold a stick. He'd been playing with bows and arrows and swords and knives while she was out and about torturing wild boars and unsuspecting passers-by as a faery child. He had found his purpose.

Her thoughts then turned to Kale. He was careful, aware of emotions and body language, and he was caring. He also knew where he belonged. Well, at least before he'd been shrunk. He had a loving family and every chance to find a wife and start his own family. He had his talent for sculpture, a bright future in his work. She had to get him back to normal. She had to re-piece the parts of his life that she'd torn apart. He'd live on, happily, and she would feel content knowing that for once, she did something right in her life.

Just thinking about it, Nahtaia was desperate to go on and make things work, to put things back where they belonged. She wanted to push herself forward with new fervor, fighting off the voices in the back of her mind that tried to take her down.

The next evening, when shadows crawled on the ground like creeping fingers, the three were just about to settle for the night when they heard voices. Nahtaia's curiosity was quickly piqued, and she hurried across the branch outstretching from the den before Oren landed nimbly ahead of her.

"Not a good idea, Bluebird," he said. Though one side of his mouth was curved in a half-smile, the seriousness in his eyes made her stop. She looked over his shoulder and bit her lip in thought.

"Who is it?" she asked him.

Oren crossed his arms over his chest and took a deep breath as he turned. "Ash pixies," he replied.

Nahtaia's eyes widened in surprise and she stumbled backward, hurrying to get deeper into the den. Oren turned with a frown at her sudden movement and followed her inside. Kale was sitting down, eating a berry that he'd picked from a nearby bush. The look on Nahtaia's face seemed to interest him.

"Pixies? Outside of the Everdark?" she hissed.

Oren lifted his shoulders and pursed his lips. "They've been leaving their territory for some years now."

"Pixies?" Kale cut in, nearly dropping the berry.

"There's a small swarm staying the night nearby," Oren explained.

At that, Kale frowned and eyed the den's entrance. "Staying the night? Where?"

Oren gestured down beyond the tree. "Down there, in the open. Birds are smart enough to know they're toxic," Oren explained.

Nahtaia sat with her knees to her chest at the farthest side of the den. She'd only run into them once in her life, and that was enough to know the risk. They were mean, horrid little creatures with black, narrow eyes that, if standing close enough, reflected like glass. Their skin was gray, and black freckles mottled their arms; freckles that dispersed the poison that would kill any creature foolish enough to try to eat them

"Nahtaia?" Kale noticed she had fallen into a thoughtful silence and made his way to her side. "Are you all right?"

She didn't respond and Oren knelt before her, turning his head to make eye contact. "Bluebird?"

"I don't want them to see me like this," she whispered.

"I don't want them to see us, period," Kale said.

"I wandered into a clearing once, where a pair of them were eating a dead mouse. They poked and prodded me, staining my clothes with blood and making fun of my hair and color. Give them a wingless faery, and I couldn't tell you what they'd do."

"Pixies are what Grandmama frightened us with when we weren't behaving."

"And so she did well," a fourth voice said. The three looked to the den entrance only to find two gangly gray pixies blocking the exit. Nahtaia could feel her blood rush to her head and pound in her ears. Kale's hand stiffened on her shoulder.

"Good evening," Oren said as he stood and faced the dark creatures, one hand smoothing his beard.

The pixies exchanged grins that revealed knife-like teeth filling their mouths. "You hear that, Mox?" the taller of the two said. "It's being polite." The shorter one called Mox—though still taller than either of the faeries and Kale—laughed in reply, saliva dribbling down its chin.

"Can we be of any service?" Oren continued, keeping his tone surprisingly casual. He crossed his arms over his chest as he often did, flexing his muscles to look larger and stronger. Though the pixies had height, Oren had brawn, and that made Nahtaia feel just a pinch better.

The taller pixie put its bony hand on its chest and bowed its head, saying, "I am Rumz. Mox and I have settled nearby with some others." It was difficult to say—since the pixies had no pupils—where their gaze fell, but Nahtaia was almost sure they were eyeing Kale. "I wonder," Rumz went on as it licked its lips, "how it is your human is so...conveniently sized?" Nahtaia and Kale exchanged glances while Oren casually put his hands behind his back to grab hold of his bow.

Oren cocked his head to the side as if truly curious as to what they meant and asked, "Conveniently?"

The pixies were having a hard time holding all of their spit in their mouths.

"He must be delicious," Rumz heaved with a step forward. Mox was trembling with a lack of self-control, its spindly fingers curled in craving desire as it stepped forward. Oren had an arrow readied in the blink of an eye, and when Mox lunged forward with a guttural cry, he released it, piercing the creature through the throat. Rumz looked down at its lifeless partner and let out a serpent-like hiss before charging at Oren. Oren wasn't ready for it. He hit the wall behind him with a loud thump. Teeth were inches away from his neck as he held it by the throat.

Nahtaia pushed Kale aside and tackled Rumz from behind. The pixie shrieked, grabbed Nahtaia's hair, and flipped her over its back. The wood of the tree cracked as she hit the ground with a cry.

A series of screams suddenly came from outside. Oren shot arrow after arrow with impossible speed and accuracy at the number of pixies trying to cram into the den, all driven by their lust for flesh, but he couldn't shoot them all. A body ran headlong into him, throwing him to the ground again.

"Oren!" Nahtaia cried, unsure of who to help first as she saw Rumz simultaneously lurching toward Kale. She met Kale's gaze for a moment when, just as Rumz leaped for the kill, he met it in the air and brought it to the ground in surprise. Nahtaia turned, snatched an arrow from the body of a dead pixie, and thrust it into the back of another that was tearing at Oren. Oren pulled an arrow from his quiver and drove it into the stomach of one pixie, then swung his leg around, knocking yet another to the ground. He rolled backward, grabbing hold of his bow and sent three arrows whistling through the air.

Kale was still wrestling with Rumz when it sank its teeth into his shoulder and he cried out in pain.

Nahtaia screamed in shock when she felt the breeze of an arrow cut the air just centimeters from her nose—it lodged in Rumz's side. The pixie stumbled back with a hiss and Oren shot it again. Rumz finally fell to the ground and stopped moving.

Death was everywhere.

Nahtaia dropped to the floor beside Kale, breathing heavily with exhaustion.

What just happened?" she asked with a groan, her eyes skimming over all the dead creatures.

Kale licked his lips and clenched his teeth in pain before replying. "I think the three of us just took on a hoard of killer pixies."

Nahtaia noticed Kale holding his shoulder as crimson blood stained his clothing. She moved his shirt from the wound to get a closer look as Oren retrieved his arrows.

"Is he all right?" Oren asked.

"It looks worse than it is," she assured them both. "Keep pressure on it, Kale."

Oren poked his head outside the entrance and looked at the trees before saying, "I'll be back," then flew away. He was back in less than a minute with a glob of tree sap on a leaf.

"Pine sap," he said, nudging Nahtaia aside. He pulled Kale's shirt away from the bite wound and slathered it with the sap. "It's antiseptic, which cleans the wound so it doesn't get infected."

Nahtaia cocked her brows. "How do you know that will work on a human?"

"Living so close to a human village, we pine fae in Lyra have to know *everything* about them. More of a precaution than anything else."

"Well, thank you," Kale said to Oren with more emotion in his eyes than Nahtaia had ever seen. He must have been as surprised as she was. It was their first bonding moment, it seemed.

Nahtaia thought back on the journey. How much knowledge was Oren hiding? She turned her attention back to the mess in the den. "How many were there?"

Oren slowly rose to his feet, counting the bodies. His eyes widened. "Twelve," he said. "There were twelve."

Nahtaia counted them herself.

Oren was right.

"How is that possible?" Kale asked.

Nahtaia and Oren looked toward the den entrance when Oren shook his head and replied, "It's not. Someone helped us."

Chapter 19

Nahtaia closed her eyes as she took a deep breath through her mouth, pausing from wrapping the sappy leaves Oren had brought around Kale's shoulder wound. The pungent stench of decaying pixies stung her nose and stimulated her gag reflex.

"Are you all right?" Kale asked, though the nasality of his own voice was apparent. Everyone was holding their breath as Oren rolled and dumped the gray bodies from the den. It didn't take much time for a pixie's body to wither and the flesh to disintegrate after it died, leaving behind relics of bone. Nahtaia shook her head and blinked away the stinging tears that brimmed. She wasn't crying, the smell was just so strong.

"I'm not sure I can sleep in here," she said, looking over her shoulder to eye the blood staining the wood where they would normally sleep. She turned and gazed pleadingly at Oren, who rolled one of the last two lifeless creatures toward the door. He stopped, as if feeling her eyes on him, and turned around.

"What?" he innocently asked.

"Can we find somewhere else to sleep?" Kale asked in Nahtaia's stead. Oren skimmed the trees of the forest and ran a hand down his chin.

"It's late," he said. "The night birds will be out." He turned back and met Nahtaia's watery eyes and frowned. He sympathized for her and was about to say he'd try to take a quick look when Nahtaia gestured passively with her hands and shook her head, saying, "I'll just sleep near the door."

When night befell the woods, it seemed darker and more sinister than usual. Every time Nahtaia closed her eyes, visions of black eyes and razor-sharp teeth filled her mind. Hearing Oren and Kale tossing and turning, she could tell they were in a similar situation.

A breeze blew into the den, taunting the three with fresh air as they tried to sleep. Nahtaia took a breath through her nose as the wind touched her face, but as soon as it faded, her stomach heaved and she swallowed the bile that rose. The entire night passed slower than any night she had experienced.

When sunlight broke through the branches and cued the night song's end, Nahtaia, Oren, and Kale hurried to the forest floor. Bones at the foot of the tree were all that remained of the pixies.

"Do you really think someone helped us?" Nahtaia asked, stealing one more glance at the corpses as the three began their traveling for the day. Oren furrowed his brow in thought and slowed to walk beside her.

"I don't see what other possibility there is," he replied. "Put one faery against one pixie and there's a chance. One faery against two pixies is a gamble. Three of us against twelve of them? Impossible."

The thought bothered Nahtaia. How could someone have helped them without being seen? "Who do you suppose it was?" she asked.

As Oren worked through his reply, Kale filled the silence when he answered, "The Voices." Nahtaia stumbled at the mention of the Great Four.

"Why would you say that?" she asked. Her heart was beating double time, though she couldn't tell whether it was due to excitement or anxiety.

"It makes sense," he sighed. "And," he paused, "I-I saw something." At that, Oren stepped out of his natural walking rhythm. His eyes seemed to ask, "What do you mean?"

"Just two nights ago," Kale went on and nodded toward Oren. "You noticed. I thought maybe you'd seen, but when you said nothing, I was afraid to mention it. I thought maybe exhaustion was getting to my head."

"Well, what did you see?" Nahtaia squealed. Her curiosity had worn her patience thin.

Kale swallowed as he pieced his words together. "You and Oren were outside of the den, talking. When he walked away, there was a glow around you, and a very subtle change in the air above your back. It took the form of wings."

Nahtaia was speechless. Oren, on the other hand, let out a skeptic's scoff.

"You were right," Oren smirked with a wrinkled brow. "Exhaustion *has* gotten to you."

Kale looked at Nahtaia, then frowned at Oren with tight lips. "I expected you not to believe me," he said, returning his attention to Nahtaia.

Nahtaia chewed her lip and wrung her hands in thought. Oren passed glances between the two and scoffed. "You can't actually believe him," he said.

"What's so hard to believe?" Kale asked, now even more irritated by Oren.

"You're just a human. You have no magic nor means of seeing anything like *we* do," he said, gesturing to Nahtaia and himself.

Kale turned his gaze forward and continued on his way as he muttered, "Maybe if you'd have paid attention…"

Oren's hand shot out and grabbed his uninjured shoulder, forcing him around. "If you have something to say, *say it*," Oren growled.

Nahtaia knew the argument wouldn't get better any time soon. How naïve of her to think their subtle bonding moment in the den the night before would mean anything in the long run of this journey.

"How about we give him the benefit of the doubt?" she suggested. "Let's think about whether it's likely for the Voices to be reaching out—"

"It's impossible, Nahtaia," Oren interrupted. "Why would he see something that I would not? I was there with him that night. Right next to him. Why wouldn't I have seen it?"

"Kale specifically said it happened when you were walking away, Oren. You weren't standing next to him. And why does it matter?" she replied. "Let's just think about this."

Oren turned with a growl and worked his hand through his hair.

"I can't believe you're getting so frustrated over something that should be taken as a good sign," Nahtaia noted.

"Why don't you just say it out loud?" Kale said in a mocking tone. "You're jealous."

Nahtaia let out a quiet gasp as Oren froze in his steps and whipped back around.

Kale went on. "I saw something meaningful instead of you. You still think just because you're 'of magic' that you're better than me."

In the blink of an eye, Oren was inches from Kale's face, but Kale stood his ground.

"Jealous?" Oren said. There was a new fire in his voice, and his flared nostrils showed the rage he was having trouble controlling.

Nahtaia squeezed in between the two and faced Kale. "Let's end this," she said. Though she was speaking to them both, the eye she gave Kale warned him to be the one to finish it. She knew Oren well enough to know that he would never let anyone make him feel small. Kale wrinkled his nose and grit his teeth.

"Now," she pressed. "I believe you, all right?"

That was not a good idea. Oren stiffened behind her and she heard his sudden intake of air. "There's nothing to believe! He's lying! He's just—" Oren paused then, then let out a short laugh of disbelief. "He's trying to get your attention again."

"What?" Kale said with a frown.

"Of course! You're trying to be some sort of hero. The bearer of good news. You know this is the one thing Nahtaia is hoping for and you're playing with her feelings."

Kale turned and stomped off before Oren finished his thought.

"Hey!" Oren shouted. "I'm talking to you!"

"No, you're going on a jealous rampage," Kale corrected.

Nahtaia couldn't believe they were getting into another fight. She thought all that was in the past and done with.

"Why should I be jealous? I *have* Nahtaia already."

Blood flooded to Nahtaia's cheeks at the declaration. Kale's step faltered but he didn't turn back. Oren only realized what he'd said wrong after the words left his lips. He turned and met Nahtaia's cold, angry glare.

"You promised," she said just loud enough for him to hear. Then she walked off after Kale.

"Nahtaia, he's being—"

"You have nothing," she called over her shoulder.

The ache in Terry's feet was bone deep and traveled up to her back. She'd walked nonstop the entire day before and most of the night. Grandmama had told her a number of times that she believed a faery city was in the woods just outside their farm. She wasn't sure if it was true, but she thought that if she at least found a faery, she'd be pointed in the right direction. Willy was sick and Kale was *not* dead—she was going crazy sitting around and doing nothing either situation.

The morning was cold in the shade of the forest canopy, so Terry pushed herself faster to warm her blood. She'd given up trying to be careful not to get dirty when, during the night, she'd tripped and fallen into a pool of mud. *Anyway*, she thought, *I'm sure faeries don't stand on ceremony.*

A flock of birds fled a tree nearby and Terry jumped in surprise at the sudden noise. She turned, skimming the length of the woods. A sense of a presence settled heavily on her shoulders. When she saw nothing, she slowly turned and walked on.

A twig crunched under the foot of something behind her. She whipped back around, her heart in her throat.

"Who's there?" she called, though her voice was weaker than she'd have liked. Images of hungry wild animals crowded her thoughts, and she knew she had little chance of fighting anything off by herself. A grunt came from the side and she spun to face that direction. She didn't want to be caught off guard.

"Please," she said to whatever it was. "I'm looking for my brother. He's with a faery. A faery with blue hair."

She heard another grunt in reply. Terry leaned on her left foot to steal a peek around a wide tree trunk and froze at the sight. Not fifty feet away stood a large bear. She stood perfectly still as it sniffed the air around it, then put its nose to the ground. She took a slow, careful step backwards and froze again when it let out a quiet growl. Swallowing an egg-sized lump in her throat, she took a breath, turned, and ran away as fast as her feet would carry her. The bear let out a monstrous roar and she could hear its heavy paws pounding with every running step.

There was a new tension between Nahtaia and her fellow travelers. Oren eventually made his way in front of Kale, and she bristled at his stubbornness, remembering why she disliked him so much over the years. He couldn't stand anything not going *his* way.

"Fool," she muttered under her breath. When she kicked a pebble, Kale looked over his shoulder. His eyes were hard but he slowed down anyway.

"I never meant for—" he started, but Nahtaia stopped him with an abrupt wave of her hand.

"Don't bother," she replied with a sigh. "Oren will only get all the more annoyed and you'll both start talking with your fists instead of your lips." Kale was about to respond but she continued, saying, "*If* the Voices *are* watching us, then whatever happens will happen according to them. That's all."

"And if they're not, and he's lying?" Oren said, inviting himself into the conversation. He stood before them with his feet shoulder-width apart and his arms across his chest, making himself look tougher than usual.

"Then we'll all die horrible deaths and all our troubles will be over," she snapped, then pushed past him. Oren narrowed his eyes at her, then shifted them to Kale, who replied in much the same way.

"I hope you're not blaming me," Kale called after her, irritation suddenly clear in his tone.

Nahtaia's steps fell hard with determination.

"I'm blaming both of you. You two don't know when to stop. All you do is fight and mock, fight and mock. I will be happy to befriend both of you after you two learn to behave like adults."

"This is coming from the one who shrank the human," Oren said matter-of-factly. Nahtaia stopped. A smile played at his lips when he saw her familiar irritated facial expression.

"If I remember well, I shrank him because *you*," she poked Oren in the chest, "interrupted the moment! Because *you* act rashly at the worst of times!"

One of Oren's eyebrows rose as did one side of his mouth in a half-smile. Nahtaia wrinkled her brow. "Stop it!" she ordered with a slap to his chest.

"Help!" a voice full of desperation called in the distance. "Help me!"

The ears of the three perked at the sound and without another word, Oren took off in the direction of the call. Nahtaia and Kale exchanged glances, then took off after him. The owner of the voice soon came into view, and Nahtaia spotted Oren in the air with an arrow already nocked.

"Terry?" Kale said from beside Nahtaia. "What is she doing out here?" The bear entered his view, and he cried, "Terry!"

Terry looked around but couldn't seem to find where her name had come from. The bear let out a pained howl and she stole a glance over her shoulder, gasping at the sight of the animal stopped and hunched over. She skidded to a halt and skimmed the area, her breaths heavy, her eyes wide. "Hello?" she said.

"Terry!" Kale called with a laugh. "Down here! On the ground!" Terry turned her attention to the ground, her gaze stopping on Nahtaia and her shrunken brother. With eyes wide and her jaw dropped, Terry kneeled on the floor in front of them.

"Kale?" she whimpered, sounding half surprised and half teary, glad to see her brother was alive. "W-what happened to you?" Just as she asked, she set her eyes on the blue faery beside him. "Nahtaia?"

"It's a long story," Kale sighed in relief.

Nahtaia stepped forward with her head hung in shame. She regretted lying to the Mason family but nothing could change what she did in the past. "Hello, Terry," Nahtaia said. Oren landed nimbly on his feet beside her, bow in hand, and realization seemed to strike Terry about what happened to the bear.

"Thank you," she said to Oren. He bowed his head in reply and she turned her attention back to her brother. "But h-how? How did this happen?"

Nahtaia turned her face to the ground, wringing her hands behind her back. "That would be my fault," she said. With a sigh, she lifted her eyes to Terry and bit her lip. "I'm sorry for everything, Terry. I never meant to hurt anyone. And this," she gestured to Kale, "was an accident."

"Nahtaia," Kale started.

"Is it fixable?" Terry asked Nahtaia.

Nahtaia swallowed hard. "Not by me. My magic is gone; I've been trying to find a way to get it back. There are other ways, though. I think."

The last bit of Nahtaia's response had concern pouring over Terry's face. "All right. We'll have to discuss this more, but for now, we have to hurry home. Willy is gravely ill." Kale stepped forward in alarm. "I came out here looking for you," his sister went on. "Nahtaia, I was hoping you could use your magic to make him better."

"What's happened to him?" Kale asked.

"He's been feverish for days. I'm afraid he only has a few days left. He's dying, Kale."

Nahtaia looked up at Oren who pressed his lips in a tight line. "Even if I did have magic," Nahtaia started, "I don't have healing powers for humans."

"But Minister Astoun does," Oren suggested. "If we can get back to Lyra, I'm sure she would be willing to lend a hand."

A memory of Astoun's healing blaze flashed in Nahtaia's mind and she winced. It wasn't exactly a pleasant feeling, but it worked for just about any injury or illness in any creature. Anxiety soon followed that thought. Nahtaia would be facing the ministers after all.

"Please," Kale begged. "We have to try. Terry can take us."

"Which way is your city?" Terry asked. Oren pointed in the direction from which she had come, and she offered her hand for Nahtaia and Kale to climb onto. They looked at one another and sat in Terry's palm, then Terry hurried them after Oren toward the faery city.

Chapter 20

It was incredible how much distance the group traveled in such short time. By nightfall, they were already in familiar territory. When Oren realized where they were, he stopped in mid-flight and spun in circles, finding it hard to believe.

"What is it?" Nahtaia asked, then Terry repeated the question louder. Oren flew down into hearing range.

"How did we get here so fast?" he asked.

Nahtaia and Kale exchanged glances, then studied their surroundings. They were less than a mile from the farm, which meant they were even closer to Lyra.

"I'm starting to think we're being aided by whoever helped us with the pixies," Kale said.

"I don't think I disagree," Oren added. "Let's keep going."

Every step closer to the city was a step closer to the ministers, and Nahtaia was losing courage. She still didn't have even the slightest clue of what would be done with her and she wasn't sure if she really wanted to know. If not for Willy being sick, she probably would have just left them now. But as much as she disliked Willy, she didn't want to see him hurt, much less die.

It wasn't long before they passed beyond the border of Lyra. Nahtaia stiffened and grit her teeth nervously. It was obvious enough for Kale to notice.

"How are you feeling?" he asked, setting a hand on her shoulder. She flashed him a flimsy smile.

"I'm all right. I think. I will be. We'll see," she mumbled, gazing up at the moonlight breaking through the trees in slivers of silver and white. She closed her eyes and took a breath when Terry stopped running. They were standing before the central oak where Lyra's ministers resided. Terry and Kale looked around, unsure of what to expect.

"Will we be able to see anything?" Terry whispered. "I mean, I know not all humans can see magic unless it's shown to us."

Nahtaia nodded and pointed to the oak as golden magic moved through the trunk, cutting a doorway that, when opened, revealed the four ministers standing shoulder to shoulder. Oren landed before them and crossed an arm over his chest with a bow. Terry put her hand down and Nahtaia stepped up beside him, gesturing as Oren just had.

"Ministers," Oren began, straightening back up again. "You've been expecting us?" The question was sincere though it sounded like more of a statement. He raised his eyebrows when they didn't reply and followed their gaze, set coldly on Nahtaia.

Moriel spoke first. "Miss Nahtaia," he began. "You have created a rift within the faery realm that will not easily heal. The humans are more than just angry with us because of your carelessness."

Before he could continue, Oren stepped forward. "With all due respect, Minister Moriel, before we speak of this and settle on any punishment or sentence, I wonder if we should send the human back to his world."

"Oren," Kale started but was cut off.

"If we wish to settle any misdealings with the surrounding humans," Oren said, "we have the greatest of opportunities as we speak."

Moriel and his fellow ministers exchanged glances. "You have my attention," he said.

Oren looked back at Terry and Kale, then took a breath. "The humans' younger brother is gravely ill. If we offer healing, I am positive the family involved in this crisis will turn their heads from all of this."

"Sir Oren," Moriel started in reply. "You do realize that stalling will not save Nahtaia in the end?"

"Yes, Moriel, I do. But I am not simply stalling. There are two things that will come from this offer. One, the humans may forgive any trespasses against them and two, they will be out of the picture as we work out our own problems. It is bad enough that these humans now know the exact location of our city, but would it be wise for them to learn any more of our ways than necessary by witnessing our dealings?"

There was a pause as Moriel thought. "You've always had a way with words." He took a breath and shook his head. Motioning to Astoun, he said, "You go with Oren to the humans and tend to the ill child, I'll deal with him when you return. Groblen, take Miss Nahtaia to the lower dungeon chambers." He leaned close to the green faery and narrowed his eyes before adding, "Do not let her out of your sight. Sentinian, come with me."

"Dungeon?" Oren said. "She doesn't need to be put in any dungeon."

Sentinian pulled Moriel aside and whispered, "I do not think it wise to put her in such a place. Remember what was decreed?"

"I know what I am doing," Moriel hissed in reply. He turned away and gestured for everyone to move on as he ordered.

It was difficult for Nahtaia to swallow. To breathe, even. She shifted her attention from Kale to Oren, unable to speak.

"This is madness, Moriel!" Oren tried, blocking the minister's way. "Not the dungeon. Give her a chance!"

"She's run out of chances," Moriel snipped. "And if you do not step away, you will suffer the same fate. But not before you help settle things with the humans. Now go."

Oren stepped close to Nahtaia and whispered, "It will be fine. I'll fix this."

Nahtaia looked up at him through a blur of tears as he tucked a strand of hair behind her ear and lightly kissed her on her forehead. Then he took off toward the farm.

"Nahtaia," Kale called, not ready to leave her yet.

Terry took an uncertain step back with Kale clutched in her hands. "I'm sorry, but Willy..." she trailed off before turning and hurrying after the faeries.

"We'll get you out!" Kale shouted and faded into the distance with his sister.

Two sentries, one on each arm, led Nahtaia after Groblen to the lower chambers. Though it was what she expected, she still couldn't fight off the fear that gripped her of what was to come.

A candle flickered against the glass of Willy's bedroom window and shadows moved as someone paced to and fro. Terry didn't hesitate to bring her miniature brother into the home with the faeries she knew Grandmama hated. Grandmama wouldn't deny help from them.

"I'm back!" Terry cried. She hurried through the halls into the bedroom where her grandparents stood beside the bed. Willy lay there, looking whiter than a ghost. He was even worse than when she left.

"I brought help," Terry said.

The moment Grandmama spotted Oren and Astoun, her eyes widened in fear.

"Grandmama, don't worry! They're going to help us," Terry explained before Grandmama could speak. "And look." She held out her hand and her grandparents' eyes widened in surprise.

"Kale?" Grandfather asked, stepping closer to have a better look. "By the Highest! What's happened to you?"

Grandmama seemed to have gone into complete shock at the sight of her grandson.

"H-how did—" she began.

"It's a long story, and we'll fix me, but how's Willy?" Kale asked.

With a hesitant turn, their eyes fell upon the small boy on the bed.

"He won't last the night," Grandmama whispered. Then she turned to the faeries and said to her granddaughter, "You said they can help."

Terry looked up to Oren and Astoun and pressed her lips in a tight line. Astoun floated close to the boy, then lifted her gaze to his grandparents.

"I can heal the boy under one condition," the wild-haired faery said. "I do it for the sake of peace. Humans of your village and the fae of Lyra have never gotten along, and I hope that by helping one of your kind, we may settle our differences."

"Whatever Nahtaia did," Oren said, motioning an apology to the minister for interrupting, "was an accident. She never meant to harm anyone."

"She is being punished severely for her actions," Astoun added.

Grandmama looked to her husband, then stepped closer to Willy. She placed a hand on the child. "He is still so young; his future is broad. He deserves more life. He deserves a chance." With a sigh, she nodded and lifted her eyes to Astoun. "If you heal him, we will spread the word of your good deeds."

Nahtaia studied the grains in the wood steps that wound down to the dungeon entrance. Though she knew the sentries escorting her, she had nothing to say. Fear chilled her blood. She'd never been in the dungeon herself, but she'd heard stories. Rats the size of rabbits were said to scurry about, eating the remains of faery prisoners long passed and nibbling on the ones yet living. Her skin crawled and erupted in a myriad of bumps.

Lerth, the sentry on her left and the more built of the two, looked down at her arm with a frown. He must have felt her skin prickle.

"I never thought I'd be leading you down here, Nahtaia," he said.

"Oh, *I* had a feeling," Greng, the sentry on her right with a broken nose replied. "Especially after the Sa—"

"Shut it, toadstool!" Lerth scolded. "Really, Nahtaia, I doubt you'll be here long," he went on in a sympathetic tone. "Moriel will come to his senses. You've never really done anything *too* horrid. Not enough to deserve *this*."

"Thank you," Nahtaia muttered. "No opinion can save me now, though."

Their steps echoed out of rhythm with the sounds of dripping water and the crackling flame of Lerth's torch. The passageway was dark and only a few stairs at a time could be seen in the light of the fire as they descended. The pungent smell of mold and earth filled Nahtaia's nostrils and made her sick to her stomach. She wouldn't last long in such a place.

When the steps came to an end, the three walked down a small walkway that led to a wooden door with iron bars over a small square cut-out. Nahtaia stiffened as Lerth set his torch on the wall and tinkered with keys.

"Lerth," Nahtaia croaked. He stopped to look down at her. "What's on the other side of this door? I mean, just so I know what to expect."

The sentries looked at each other before he replied, "The shackling area. Then there's another door like this one. That's the one that opens to the dungeon." He turned his attention back to his keys and opened the door. Greng led her inside while his partner lit three other torches that brightened the room, revealing a scene that made the situation more frighteningly real.

Shackles and chains hung on every wall and in every size. All sorts of metals were used that Nahtaia never imagined the fae even knew about; metal like Kale's tools. Lerth chose the smallest pair of shackles he could find and motioned to Greng to hold her still. She cringed as she heard the chains pass through the metal rings of the shackles around her wrists in front of her, then a loud click nearly stopped her heart.

When she was chained and ready to pass into the next room, Nahtaia had to hold her breath to keep from breaking down. On the other side of the door was likely what she would see for the rest of her life.

No more hopes. No more dreams. They would be useless from here on out. Just darkness and cold and the deafening sound of silence, save for the clinks and screeches of the chains. Lerth searched through his keys again and chose the largest of the bunch. He put it into the lock, lifted sad eyes to Nahtaia, then pushed the door open.

A whoosh of crisp, fresh air came from the other side along with a light so bright the three faeries recoiled and shielded their eyes. A sound like that of laughter hovered in the air before them and a voice spoke.

"Come, little troublemaker. It's time we met face to face."

Chapter 21

With arms crossed and his bow securely in his grip, Oren looked down at the limp body of Willeim Mason with little to no sympathy. He *was* the boy who started all the trouble by capturing Nahtaia in the first place. Sure, it also opened the door for him and Nahtaia to be together, but still. He was confident it would have happened with or without their adventure to the elves.

Minister Astoun hovered over the bedraggled boy, arms outstretched. The palms of her hands expelled from them an eerie glow of healing magic. Light curled toward the boy like a tongue of smoke and expanded until his body was enveloped by it. His fingers first twitched, then his arms until his body began to shudder and his breaths were rapid.

Oren shifted his attention to the grandmother, who looked suspicious and afraid. The elderly woman's husband pulled her comfortingly to his chest. *He seems more trustworthy than she*, Oren thought. Seeing the old couple together and so in love brought a small smile to Oren's face as he pondered on Nahtaia. That smile quickly faded as he remembered where she was. Was she really reduced to a prisoner? How badly was she suffering? He ached to get her out of such a place.

Willy's body jerked and trembled as the magic touched his illness. It was hard to tell if the boy was conscious enough to feel the healing or if it was just his body reacting. Nearly every faery of Lyra had a healing experience with Astoun and it was never pleasant, but Willy showed no sign of discomfort. With the final touch of magic, color returned to his face.

A smile wrinkled the elderly man's face as he gently gestured to his wife. She turned to look at their grandchild, who lay sleeping peacefully and looking healthier than he had in weeks. Sweat dampened his hairline, but it was clear that he was going to be all right. The woman looked to the faeries and Oren creased his brow in wonder. A new sensation came from the woman. A renewed light shone in her eyes, and even though she was unable to speak through her sniffles and streaming tears, it was clear that the emotion in her eyes was of pure love and thankfulness. It was difficult then to think so negatively upon the humans.

"It is finished," Astoun declared as she turned to the humans. "Our part is done and we will now return to our home. I expect you will hold to your part of the agreement. Faeries will remain out of human territory as much as the powers of the faery realm can hold them back."

The old woman stepped forward, clutching a handkerchief to her chest.

"You saved Willeim," she sobbed. "You are welcome to our home any time you—"

"No!" Astoun shrieked, throwing her hands up in a silencing gesture. "Say no such thing! Nahtaia has been more than enough trouble. We needn't have any more follow in her footsteps. We thank you and wish you well." The minister turned to Oren and motioned to him to follow.

"Wait!" Kale called. "What about me? How am I going to return to normal?"

Oren turned to Astoun, expecting she would have the answer.

"By dawn, you will return to your natural state," the minister replied.

Grandmama stepped forward. "You're certain?"

Minister Astoun bowed her head and said, "By the Highest Power, I swear it." The elderly couple nodded in understanding and looked to Kale, who stood up and stepped toward Oren. He ran a hand through his hair and took a deep breath, gathering his thoughts.

"It's been quite an adventure with you," Kale said.

Oren stood straight as usual with his arms crossed over his chest. He looked Kale over and allowed one side of his lips to curve up into a half-smile.

"It has," Oren replied. He held out his hand, which Kale accepted and shook.

"Take care of Nahtaia."

"I'll do what I can. With Nahtaia, no one knows what the future holds." Oren bowed his head to the humans, looked once more upon Willy, and took off after Astoun.

From a dark, damp dungeon full of promises of suffering and death, Nahtaia stepped into a grassy meadow. The shackles unlocked and fell to the floor. Lerth and Greng, who followed hesitantly behind, didn't bother trying to replace them.

Wildflowers swayed in a cool breeze that smelled of lilac and calmed the faeries' senses. Nahtaia looked back at the sentries whose faces held no hope of an answer as to what happened to the dungeon.

"Men of the faery realm," the words were not spoken with a solid voice but as a whisper on a new breeze. "Return to your world."

Lerth and Greng exchanged disappointed glances, then when a strong wind blew against them, hurried back from where they came. Nahtaia swallowed hard, not sure whether she was nervous or glad to see them leave. She was alone now. Just her and the strange voice that seemed to speak from all directions at once.

"Do not fear me, Moon Faery Nahtaia. Come forward and all your questions will be answered."

Nahtaia was silent as she continued on; a massive windmill came into focus before her like a mountain peak through dispersing morning fog—it was a windmill of Mae'Ehr. She hurried and couldn't help but sob the moment she caught sight of the young woman sitting atop a rising stone beside the windmill. Curls of gold spiraled down her back and shoulders, matching perfectly with her yellow eyes.

Poette dropped down from the stone and walked to the weeping blue faery. Every step made her smaller until she was the same size as Nahtaia.

Nahtaia hurried to the Voice and couldn't stop herself from throwing her arms around her waist. She felt like a child crying in her mother's embrace. The Voice laughed as she smoothed Nahtaia's hair.

Nahtaia looked up, embarrassed at her rash reaction. "I'm sorry," she sniffled. "I've just—"

"You've just been through much difficulty," Poette replied, finishing her thought. "But it was never as hopeless as you feared."

Nahtaia frowned, not understanding what the Voice was saying.

"My sister Voices and I have been watching you since before your adventure. You first caught our attention when we heard the cries of help from a minotaur."

Blood heated Nahtaia's face as she wondered why charming the bull was her most popular performance. She'd done worse in her time.

Poette continued. "We could hardly believe our eyes when we saw such a fiery little faery being the cause of such distress. And then," the Voice's eyes distanced as she thought back, "and then we saw you with that adorable pine faery, Oren, and even as the Voices of Jaydür, we could not settle our ideas on what could come from you two. We wanted to see if you would continue to struggle against one another or fall in love, and we swore to one another that we would not intervene unless it was for your life." Poette let out a giggle, then quickly brought her fingers to her lips. "Then Kale. That poor, poor human," she laughed. "He had no idea. But you know, in my opinion, humans have never really had the tendency to want what is good for them."

Nahtaia listened intently as the Voice spoke. She'd been watched all this time? The thought bothered her. Why did they let her suffer if they enjoyed her so much? Some of her questions needed to be answered.

"You mean," she began in a small voice, "that all this time, you were sitting back and watching as I searched for the Voice of D'Irdda? All this time, you all knew how much trouble I was in?" Her voice began to rise with her tension. "All this time, you had it in mind to help me?"

The soft features of Poette's face made it hard to be angry. The Voice tilted Nahtaia's face up to look her in the eyes and said, "Troubles help you grow, and you most definitely needed some growing." She dropped her hand from Nahtaia. "And besides, even a Voice needs some fun, little one."

"That's not fair," Nahtaia whispered.

"Would you rather have been alone and in danger all that time? Because by all means, I could always—"

"No!" Nahtaia cried. "No! I'm glad, of course, that everything is fine. Thank you. It's just, after all this stress..."

"You've learned and you've changed, Nahtaia. In such a short time, you've grown more than some do in a lifetime. And—" she paused, stood straight, and looked at the faery from the corner of her eyes. "We're not finished with you yet."

With that, Nahtaia bristled to attention, huffing and puffing in annoyance. "What do you mean? There can't possibly be more to suffer!"

Poette arched an eyebrow with a smile. "Did I say suffer?"

Nahtaia waited for an explanation. If she wasn't going to suffer, what was she going to be used for?

As if aware of her thoughts, Poette giggled and said, "You have a great destiny ahead of you. You've matured in such a way that you are deemed worthy and useful to us Voices. You see, this was all a test. You will be called upon, though you may not realize it at the time. It is all part of learning from this life, dear one." Poette clasped her hands and her eyes lit up in excitement. "Now, for another turn of events."

"Nahtaia!" a voice called from behind. Nahtaia turned and found Oren flying toward her from the distance. She practically leaped into his arms the moment he was within reach.

"What is this? Where are we?" He paused before exclaiming, "Your wings!" Nahtaia's eyes widened and she looked over her shoulders to see translucent wings fluttering from her back.

"By the Highest!" she squealed, spinning in circles as if she could see them better if she moved fast enough. "My wings are back! Oren, my wings are back!"

Oren's excitement over her wings was short-lived. Nahtaia stopped to see Oren's jaw drop and his attention fully on Poette.

"Am I dreaming?" he asked just before bowing his head and crossing his arm over his chest, as was custom for the fae. "Great Voice," he stammered. "It is a great pleasure to—"

"Oh, stop it, Oren," Poette giggled. "Let me see you together."

Oren stood back up and smiled down at Nahtaia, stroking her cheek with a finger.

"You wouldn't believe what she's told me," Nahtaia said to him.

"I was properly informed on the way here," Oren replied. "Moriel wasn't supposed to punish you. All that's happened is because of the Voices." He looked up to Poette and grinned. "And that means, I have *you* to thank for everything."

Nahtaia blushed at his words, then her mind flashed a reminder of the other half of their problems.

"What about Kale?" she asked in a hurry. "Is he still shrunken?"

"I will take care of that," Poette replied. "What I am curious about though," she continued as she put her hands behind her back and bit her lip, trying to hide her smile, "is whether this means you two will stay together?"

Nahtaia and Oren looked one another in the eyes.

"*I* hope so," Oren said. "If she will have me."

Nahtaia blushed as the two stared expectantly at her, waiting for an answer. She licked her lips and thought on what life was going to be like from then on. She couldn't imagine not having Oren around, and yet she was never able to imagine them together. "There's no better way to find out if it'll work than to give it a chance." She mirrored Oren's half-smile. "We'll see how long we get along," she teased.

Terry placed Kale on the windowsill to look out at the dark night. He was waiting to be changed back but more than that, he was hoping to see the glow of the fae at the edge of the woods. Would Nahtaia ever come back? Life seemed too quiet and boring already, and his future didn't seem as bright as it once did. What was he going to do for the rest of his life? Continue with stone carving? Though that answer was more likely than any other, he missed the feeling of adventure and knew the emotion would only worsen with time. Maybe he would become a Wanderer of Jaydür.

"Kale," Terry said. "Are you all right?"

Turning to his sister, he smiled. "I will be."

She sat on the floor by the window, folding her arms over the sill beside her brother. "Nahtaia is good, right?" she asked, looking up at the stars. "I mean, she's not evil."

Kale chuckled and looked up at the now full moon. "No, she's not evil."

"Was she anything she seemed while she was with us?"

With his brow furrowed in thought, Kale laughed. "No. She's nothing like we thought. She's ill-tempered, impatient, pushy, and has no idea what she wants."

Terry pressed her lips tightly together and sighed. "But you love her?" Her brother's smile faded at the words.

"I will always hold a place for her in my heart," he replied. "But it would never have worked out. It took some time to realize but I've settled on it. Whoever remains with Nahtaia will have to remain with Oren. I'd never agree to a life like that."

"The green faery?" Terry questioned.

Just as he was about to answer, Kale's body tingled as if it were asleep all over. His muscles twitched and his arms and legs stretched until he reached his natural size.

Terry stepped back until she was sure he was finished growing and then threw her arms around her brother's neck. "By the Highest Power!" she cried. "Grandmama! Kale's back to normal!"

Grandmama, Grandfather, and little Willy hurried into the room to see with their own eyes. The family came together and embraced, then Willy pulled back and said, "So, will you believe me next time a girl who's secretly a faery comes to our house?"

Kale's eyes widened in exasperation. "Boy, I think you'd be better off keeping your eyes shut from now on. No more faeries," he laughed.

"Not in our house, at least," Terry added. "But you have some adventures to share with us."

Kale passed one more glance up at the moon, then grinned. "You'll have to sit for this one. It may take all night...and then some."

Chapter 22

Nahtaia, wait!" Oren called from behind.

Nahtaia looked over her shoulder as he dodged twigs and branches in pursuit of her. Her lips pulled into a half-smile and she slowed her flight as she neared the forest's edge.

"And here I thought you'd learned to keep up with me, Oren," she teased in reply.

Oren stopped beside her. "What do you think you're doing? Don't you remember what happened last time? The ministers will have you for dinner if they find out what you're up to."

"I just want to check on Kale!" Nahtaia replied with wide, innocent eyes. "I won't even talk to him," she said, passing a quick glance through the trees behind Oren. She wasn't sure whether or not Moriel had secret sentries following her since her return. She would not have been surprised, however, if he'd gone that far. "It's been a long time."

"Maybe it's better that way," Oren said. "Let him get his life back together. Let him—"

Nahtaia hovered toward him until she was inches from his face. "Are you being jealous again?" The grin that spread on her face quickly broke the seriousness of Oren's.

Oren took her hand, and she didn't resist. "I have every right to be jealous. He almost had your heart." With his last word, Nahtaia leaned in and stole a kiss before turning and flying toward the farmhouse. Just as she was about to leave the line of trees of the forest, Oren snatched her by the ankle and pulled her in the cover of a shrub. A horse trotted up to the house, pulling a cart behind it. A girl, not much older than her, sat in the cart with an older man beside her. She held a bonnet on her blonde head with a thin, delicate hand. She was rather pretty for a human girl. When the cart stopped before the home, Grandmama stepped out with her hands clasped at her mouth, a smile hiding behind them.

"Welcome!" she said as the older man assisted the girl in climbing down from the cart. "Come in! It is such a pleasure to see you two again. I pray the Missus is well? It's a pity she could not make the trip herself. Well, come in! The table is set!"

The girl wore a simple though elegant ivory dress that dropped just an inch from the floor. There was a movement by the door and Nahtaia saw Kale, dressed in odd clothes she'd never seen before. He looked quite elegant himself.

The girl stopped and smiled generously at Kale as he stepped confidently toward her. Nahtaia watched in wonder as the two exchanged some words and walked into the home. Nahtaia narrowed her eyes in curiosity and flitted to the window that opened to the kitchen, remaining unseen below the sill. With a glance over her shoulder, she saw Oren in the shrub, shaking his head in exasperation.

Nahtaia turned her head to hear better.

"Two years have changed you, Lyla," Grandfather said. "You've grown."

"In beauty, might I add," Grandmama said. It was obvious she spoke through a smile. "Your mother would be proud. I fondly think of the days you, Kale, and Terry spent beside the creek when you were younger."

Nahtaia thought hard on whether or not she remembered Kale speaking of any girl named Lyla. It didn't ring any bells of memory. She noticed the human girl sitting with her hands folded on her lap. Kale sat across from her, a smile flirting across his lips. It was his attention, though, that caught Nahtaia's eye. His gaze was drawn to the girl like a bee to flowers. His eyes held such a glow that she'd only seen when they spent their time together at his workplace. Only this time, he knew the girl and she knew him.

Nahtaia let go of the window and fluttered down to the ground in thought. Her heart ached to be able to speak to him again. They'd been through so much together, but Oren was right. Maybe it was better this way. He obviously had his eyes on a new girl, someone better for him, and she did not want to taint anything that may be his future happiness. Nahtaia was with Oren—with a faery, as she should be. Kale would likely remain with his own kind as well. He had feelings for Nahtaia in the past and appearing again may bring something back.

"It *is* better this way," she whispered to herself. She gazed at the ground and spotted a gray stone. Picking it up, she smiled as she focused on it in her hands. It grew slightly and curved on two ends, distorting into a crescent. Nahtaia twisted the stone in the center, carving with her magic the words "Thank you." She studied her work, flew to another window that opened into the boys' room, and set it on the windowsill where he could not miss it. With one last look back, she turned to make her way back to Oren.

"Faery," a voice called, freezing Nahtaia in mid-flight. She looked over her shoulder and set her eyes on Willy. "What's this?"

"It's a token of friendship for your family," she replied. "Please make sure Kale sees it."

Willy eyed the stone and pressed his lips in a tight line. "You know, wandering around here can get you caught."

Nahtaia bit her lip, holding back her temper that she learned never brought the best outcome.

"That depends on who knows I'm out here. Not that I'm not keen enough now to pay attention to my surroundings—or the little rats within them."

"Just a harmless warning," the boy said. "I'll be sure to get this to Kale." Nahtaia was about to move on when he added, "And, faery?" She turned and met the boy's gaze, waiting for him to continue. "Will we ever see you again?" he asked.

She thought for a moment and bared her teeth at him in jest. "There's always room for revenge, Willeim Mason."

The boy smiled back and watched as the glow of the moon faery disappeared into the woods.

"Revenge, huh?" Oren chuckled as Nahtaia returned.

"Don't worry," she replied, slowly making her way back toward the safe barrier. "I wasn't serious. I *did* learn something from our adventure. I've changed. I've grown. I've matured."

Oren took her hand and flashed her a grin when she stopped flying, her eyes narrow and her nostrils flared. He followed her gaze to a small patch of something on the ground below a large oak; a toadstool ring.

"Oh, no," Oren muttered.

"My ring!" Nahtaia shrieked. "It's been trampled!" She hurried over and perched atop a half-fallen toadstool. "Who could have done this?"

Oren landed before her and shook his head. "It could have been an accident," he said.

Nahtaia's eyes widened and she shoved him to the side as he was standing on a hoof print.

"Nahtaia," Oren tried, putting his hands up in a gesture to calm her down. "Don't do anything rash."

"That dim-witted bull!" she hissed. "He did this! Fool of a cow, I'm going to wring his neck and—" Her words trailed off as she took off into the woods in search of the minotaur.

Oren stood for a moment, taking in a breath of the fresh air. He sighed and pressed his lips tight and looked up into the canopy with a nod.

"And so life goes on." The bone-chilling roar of a minotaur shook the ground beneath him. "Nahtaia!"

Note from the Author

To my readers:

This is the final destination for *Nahtaia: A Jaydürian Adventure*. This story began as an intro to the world of Jaydür, back in the year 2010, and after a year of being published as a Wattpad Edition, I am able to look at this book with more pride than I ever thought possible.

Millions of reads, and thousands of comments opened the door to my writing career, and it's all because of you! (And this crazy moon-faery). I am thankful for all of my readers and all of those who left a review on this story at Amazon (dot) com.

One of the best ways to help an author is by leaving reviews and telling others about a book. They're simple things to do, but extremely helpful!

Thank you again, my readers.

Lilian Oake

P.S.
I have two other short stories that take place in Jaydür! Go check them out and leave a review for them as well!

The Bounty of the Everdark
An Ogre's Tale

Also read
The Dragon Cager, which is a story outside of Jaydür.